Mara W. Cohen Ioannides

We Are in Exile Estamos En Galut

Mara W. Cohen Ioannides

We Are in Exile Estamos En Galut

A Novel

Hadassa Novel

Impressum / Imprint

Bibliografische Information der Deutschen Nationalbibliothek: Die Deutsche Nationalbibliothek verzeichnet diese Publikation in der Deutschen Nationalbibliografie; detaillierte bibliografische Daten sind im Internet über http://dnb.d-nb.de abrufbar.

Bibliographic information published by the Deutsche Nationalbibliothek: The Deutsche Nationalbibliothek lists this publication in the Deutsche Nationalbibliografie; detailed bibliographic data are available in the Internet at http://dnb.d-nb.de.

Coverbild / Cover image: www.ingimage.com

Verlag / Publisher:
Hadassa Word Press
ist ein Imprint der / is a trademark of
OmniScriptum GmbH & Co. KG
Bahnhofstraße 28, 66111 Saarbrücken, Deutschland / Germany
Email: info@omniscriptum.com

Herstellung: siehe letzte Seite /
Printed at: see last page
ISBN: 978-3-639-79487-8

Acknowledgements

Research to produce an historical fiction as accurate as this is terribly important. This book owes as much to those scholars as it does to my writing and those who read the various drafts. One cannot study the *Rhodelisi* in Rhodes without the tombs of the field: Rebecca Amato Levy's memoir *I Remember Rhodes* that covers everything from folk custom to personal reminiscences; Marc D. Angel's *The Jews of Rhodes: The History of A Sephardic Community* that documents the entire history of the community, *Voices in Exile: A Study in Sephardic Intellectual History*, and *A Sephardic Passover Haggadah*; Isaac Jack Lévy's memoir *Jewish Rhodes: A Lost Culture* that provides wonderful insight into the history and culture of the Rhodelisi; and Elli Kohen and Dahlia Kohen-Gorden's *Ladino-English/English-Ladino Concise Encyclopedic Dictionary*. There is also the Voice of the Turtle's CD *Under Aegean Moons: Music of the Spanish Jews of Rhodes and Salonika* that provided not only inspiration, but the titles and words to a number of the songs mentioned in this book. The *Rhodelisi* diaspora is carefully examined by Yitzchak Kerem in a pair of articles and Gregory Viens' documentary *Island of Roses: The Jews of Rhodes in Los Angeles* makes much of what Levy writes about far more human by showing the actions. A short, but informative essay by Mark L. Berch, "Havdalah," highlights the different practices between the Ashkenazim and Sephardim. Nicholas Stavroulakis and Timothey DeVinney's *Jewish Sites and Synagogues of Greece*, along with The Rhodes Jewish Historical Foundation's website provides wonderful information about *Kahal Kadosh Shalom*.

    A number of people have been immense help as well in the creation of this book. Marcia Haddad Ikonomopoulos, the curator of the museum at Kehilah Kadosha Janina in New York City, has an immense amount of knowledge and connections that she shares most willingly. As has Yitzchak

Kerem of Hebrew University in Jerusalem and University of Thessolaniki in Greece and Stella Levi a *Rhodelisi*. The cover art was specially done for this book by the calligrapher Stephen M. Cohen, a member of Philadelphia's Calligrapher's Society. It is always a pleasure to work with him and I am thankful he had time to fit this project in. His portrayal of the courtyard of Kahal Shalom is accurate and beautiful. A special thanks to my friends Susan Atteberry Smith for proofing the manuscript, Cherri Jones for reading an early draft and encouraging me to get this published, my daughter Sasha who inspired me to write fiction about Greek Jews, and my husband Robert who saw me through the joys and sorrow of this manuscript.

I

Dora woke up and lay in bed listening. At first all she heard was her older sister Hannah's breathing next to her in bed. Then she heard Alejandro's breathing in the cot against the other wall. She reached with her ears and heard her grandmother in the kitchen. It was easy to distinguish her grandmother from her mother because of the clinking of her grandmother's *maniyas de tchaton*.

Long ago, before Dora was born, even before her father and his sisters and brothers were born, her grandfather, David, had started giving her grandmother, Hannah, these gold bracelets: sometimes as a surprise, sometimes for an occasion, like the engraved one *Nána* had when father's oldest brother was born. *Nána* Hannah told Dora, Hannah, and Alejandro stories about each bracelet. Of one thing Dora was certain, *Nóno* David had loved *Nána* Hannah very much because not only did she have many bracelets, but they were extraordinarily beautiful.

It was the clinking of these bracelets that Dora heard every morning. Her mother had only a few bracelets. That didn't mean *Bábu* loved *Mame* less than *Nóno* David had loved *Nána* Hannah, rather that the family's grocery wasn't doing as well.

The three children stretched and grumbled as they slowly awoke.

"Dora!" groaned Hannah as Dora rolled out of bed, "do not toss the cover so far back. You let the cold air in."

"What," was Dora's muffled reply as she struggled to get her nightgown over her head.

Alejandro stirred, "I am not getting up. It is too cold!" A pair of socks sailed across the room and thumped him on the head. He broke out in giggles and snatched them from the covers.

Dora stood in the middle of the room, shivering in her stockings and black dress with crisp white collar and cuffs.

3

"Hannah, come on. We cannot be late for school." Alejandro leapt out of bed and, dressed in his nightshirt and socks, dashed across the room to pull the cover off his sisters' bed. Hannah sat bolt upright and grabbed for her blanket. She caught the corner, but Alejandro kept on pulling and she was pulled along with it, landing on the floor. The three broke into hysterical laughter. As Dora wiped away her tears, she finished putting on her school uniform. Her sister and brother did the same.

Then they dashed into the kitchen for breakfast. Their shoes were warming by the fire – a special treat their *Nána* Hannah did for them. Slowly, Dora put her feet in her shoes and savored the warmth as it spread through her body. She loved these shoes. *Nána* Hannah had taken her to buy them. Not every girl in her class had new shoes every year. There were even a few girls who didn't have any, but her grandmother saved all year so she, her sister, and brother could each have shoes. To Dora, these shoes were her grandmother's love.

What she didn't know was what these shoes signified to her grandmother. *Nána* Hannah thought fond, sad thoughts of her two grandsons, David and Hiam, so far away in a place called Atlanta, Georgia. When they had left, when they hugged their grandmother goodbye with tears in their eyes, they asked her to make sure their little sisters and brother finished school. That was their only chance for a future. She had promised. Every morning, the action of warming her grandchildren's shoes reminded her of those two far away and of her promise. She knew the value of these shoes; the shoes were the symbol of education. It was the one thing she could do to help with the children's education. She had never gone to school, never learned to read. Girls didn't when she was young, but she understood the importance of it all and was pleased when she discovered her daughter-in-law, Miriam, could read and write. *Nána* Hannah believed herself too old to learn to read, but had Miriam read her the paper every evening translating the Italian into *Ladino*, while she cleaned the kitchen. Once a month *El Boletin* was published and Miriam didn't have to translate this *Ladino* paper for her mother-in-law. Everyone in the family would savor the articles in *El Boletin* because it not only covered Jewish news, but local politics from the perspective of the *Juderia*. Dora would sit at the *sofah* doing her homework and listen to her mother read the newspaper.

4

Nána Hannah bought these shoes with her piece of the money that Dora's two older brothers sent from America. She also earned a little money by sewing. She was quick and handy with a needle and thread and so many women in the *Juderea* come to her, rather than the tailor. They weren't afraid to appear to be immodest, standing in the kitchen as *Nána* Hannah tucked in their dresses or turned up a hem. Besides, they could gossip, get advice, and have a cup of coffee.

Nána Hannah did this, because of the shoes. Certainly, there wasn't spare time. There were three children to mind and cooking and housework to do; and she was far from young. Her son and daughter-in-law ran the family grocery, which was increasingly difficult as the island of Rhodes became poorer. The family had never been wealthy, but they'd always done okay.

Dora savored the warmth of her shoes and her grandmother's love, without any knowledge of her grandmother's sacrifices. She knew, though, that she was lucky. Many of their friends came to school hungry, and some couldn't come on the coldest or wettest days because they had no coats or shoes. However, she and Hannah and Alejandro went every day no matter the weather with breakfast in their stomachs, shoes on their feet, and coats to cover their backs.

The three children ate their breakfast of feta, olives, and pita as their grandmother finished cleaning the kitchen.

"Alejandro, finish what is on your plate. You cannot be hungry while you study," coaxed their grandmother. "And Dora, wipe those crumbs off your skirt. What would your teacher think if you arrived so messy at school?" Each child quickly brushed off their sweaters and grabbed their coats. As they did this, they kissed their grandmother good-bye. "Have a good day, children. Learn something!" she called after them.

"We will," they responded as they hurried through the streets to Kisthiniou Street and then to their school: *L'Alliance Israélite Universelle*.

II

"See Dora, we are not late. You always make us run here," chided Hannah as they walked through the gate of the school. "Now, Alejandro, be good in class. Listen carefully. And we will meet you here when we finish school."

"Yes, *Mame*," Alejandro teased as he turned towards the boys' building.

Hannah and Dora turned towards the girls' building.

"Did you get your homework done last night?" asked Hannah.

"Why do you ask? You are not *Mame* or *Nána* Hannah," retorted Dora.

"I just wanted to know. I know how you hate history," responded Hannah.

"I did my history, though I would rather study Italian like you. That language is so romantic, like music on my ear, and Italy sounds so exciting," Dora replied.

"Oh, no! English, study English. Who cares about romance, when one can have some money," returned Hannah. "Besides, if we learn English then we can go live with *Hermano* and Hiam."

"But I do not want to go to America and live with David and Hiam. I want to stay here with *Mame*, *Bábu*, and *Nána* Hannah," cried Dora. "How could you leave them?"

"How can we stay, silly girl?" answered Hannah. "There is no money here. We live almost entirely on what our brothers send us. Oh, there is the bell. We better hurry." At that moment they heard the ringing of the hand bell that was used to announce the start of the school day, so they rushed into the building and to their classrooms.

When the day was over they met again at the gate, amid the screaming and crying of the other children. Mostly, they heard *Ladino*. However, there was some Italian mixed in. In the last few years, the Italians insisted the language be taught in the school as a way of showing their rule of the island; thus, the children were forbidden to speak *Ladino* in the school, supposedly on the grounds as well. However, the gate was neutral and the children returned to *Ladino* there. Besides, even though most of the children in the school were Jewish, there were a few Christian boys whose fathers were Italian government officials and *La Allianca* was the best school on the island.

Dora grabbed Alejandro's hand, "Come little brother, we need to hurry home – it is *Shabbat* tonight." She wasn't the only one who was rounding up younger siblings and rushing home to help prepare for *Shabbat.*

III

Fridays were Dora's favorite day of the week. School let out early so that the children could prepare for *Shabbat*. Alejandro would play with his friends around the well on *Calle Ancha*. Sometimes they would help the women get the water or carry home their *Shabbat* packages. However, Dora and Hannah hurried home to help *Nána* Hannah.

When they arrived in the clean smelling house, they could always hear *Nána* Hannah singing old Spanish ballads as she finished the ironing. These ballads *Nána* Hannah had learned from her grandmother and she from hers. Dora's favorite was "*Yaakov le disho o Yosef*" ("Jacob said to Joseph"). Dora dropped her books on the table by the door and ran across the kitchen to hug her grandmother, wrapping her arms around her grandmother's waist and resting her head on her back. From here, Dora could feel the song in *Nána* Hannah, not just hear it. *Nána* Hannah smiled, swaying in rhythm to her song that powered her ironing.

Pronto le disho Yosef,	"At once," said Joseph,
por el tu komando.	"as you request."
Buenoz diaz, ya lez dio,	"Good day," he wished
i a todo suz ermonoz.	To all his brothers.
Presto presto kitaldi	Quickly they removed
La kamiz de arriva,	the coat he wore,
porke a Yosef ya arrelumbrava	because Joseph already shone
a la luz de dia.	As the light of the day.
A la karavana ke paso	To the passing caravan
A Yosef vendyeron	they sold him;
En caza de Potifar	to the house of Potifar
Por esklavo lo dyeron.	they gave him as a slave.

Hannah followed her sister into the house grabbing the dropped books on the way in.

"Dora, everyday I collect these. For once, especially on *Shabbat* could you remember to put your schoolbooks away," she nagged without regard to her grandmother's song.

"Hush, child," reprimanded her grandmother. "*Shabbat* comes soon. We need peace in the house." Hannah hung her head. It was rare that her grandmother reprimanded anyone. "Now children, time for us to finish *Shabbat* preparations. Hannah, please begin at the back of the house and sweep. Every corner, my dear. Do not leave any speck behind." Hannah smiled; she received the same admonition every Friday afternoon. "Dora, my dove," continued their grandmother, "put these clean clothes away. Do not forget to take out everyone's *Shabbat* clothes, including those for the table."

Dora loved this job. It gave her the opportunity to go through her grandmother's *baoul*. As she reverently lifted the wooden and metal lid, Dora remembered when she was little and she and her grandmother would spend time together looking through the trunk. In there were precious items. Inside the velvet lined box was the outfit *Nána* Hannah was married in, which she now wore for every holy day and wedding. There was a pillow cover, well worn, embroidered by *Nána* Hannah's mother. And there was the dress her brothers, father and uncles, and *Nóno* David and his brothers had worn for their *brit milot*. *Nána* Hannah kept it for her great-grandsons.

Then Dora could sneak a peek into her mother's *baoul*. This wasn't exactly approved of, but Dora was careful not to disturb anything. After she removed her mother's *Shabbat* outfit and head covering, then she would peek at her mother's wedding outfit and some items her mother had brought from her home. Then she put away the other fresh cleaned items and took out their *Shabbat* clothes. *Nána* Hannah wore traditional clothes every day of the week: a *chinatian*, *sayo*, *patuklas*, and a *yazma* around her head. On her feet were wooden *tacos*. During the week Miriam wore a *dishabille*, long skirt, thick cotton stockings and a shawl, but on *Shabbat* she and her mother-in-law dressed in a more formal version of traditional dress. While the outfit began with the *chinatian*, over this went a *breshin*, then an *anteri* followed by a *polka de samara*. Around their waists were embroidered velvet belts and around their necks were their gold chains

9

bound with a *yardans*. They pulled their hair back with a *tarposhes* and on their heads were velvet caps with a broaches pinned to sit between their eyes. They both had special slippers, as well.

Once her mother had explained it to Dora, "I do this to honor our past. My *Mame* and *Bábu's* mother wear clothes like this because that is who they are. I wear them to honor who they are and who their mothers were and their mothers as far back as we can remember."

When the two girls met up in the kitchen again, their grandmother had just sat down for a moment. The girls dragged the *paila* from the corner of the room. Carefully, *Nána* Hannah and her namesake carried pots of boiling water to the *paila*. One *Shabbat* a month and this happened to be the one, Miriam and Moses splurged on the public baths for themselves. Thus, their *Nána* bathed the children at home, so the girls could have their favorite time with their grandmother. As the *paila* filled, Dora gathered the towels and sponges and soap.

"*Nána*, where is your towel?" she called out.

"It should be on the end of my bed, dear," was *Nána's* measured reply.

Hannah stopped her *Nána* on her way to refill her pot.

"We have filled the tub, *Nána*. You can take your bath." To offer a bit of modesty, the girls turned their backs and she undressed. When they heard the delicate splash of water as she sat down, they turned around. Now they took their places sitting by the tub, knees pulled up with their chins resting on them. *Nána* Hannah sank as far into the tub as she could; the water rose to her neck and her knees stuck out.

"*Nána* Hannah, tell us a story of when you were young," the girls begged in a chorus.

"When I was young? Heavens, was I ever? I do not remember that," teased their grandmother.

"But *Nána* ...," cried the girls in unison laughing with her.

IV

"When I was not much older than you, Hannah, my parents started arranging a marriage for me," began their *Nána*. "I was only 13 and not ready yet, but my parents wanted to take their time and find me a good, honest, caring, wealthy man. They did not care if he lived in the city or the country, but I did. I did not want to be a farmer's wife. I did not want to live far from the Jewish community and only see my family for the holidays. But my *bábu*, he just wanted to make sure all his children would eat well. Come, Dora, scrub my back." Dutifully, Dora took a sponge and some soap and scrubbed her grandmother's back as the story continued.

"Many families came to my *bábu* to offer their sons. My *bábu*, while not a rabbi, was a learned man and a baker. My *mame* was well known for her cooking and embroidery. These families saw this as a good match for their son. Some families my *bábu* refused out right. No blacksmith for his only daughter. No poor farmer. Others he questioned at length and visited. There was a student of Rabbi Raphael Yitzhak Israel, the Chief Rabbi at the time, who brought a letter from his father. My *bábu* visited the family this student was living with a number of times. He also asked some of the men he bought from to ask at the island this boy was from. I do not know what happened, but that boy went home without me."

"There now," paused their grandmother, "I think I am done. Hand me a towel Hannah and in you go." Quickly, Hannah undressed and climbed in the warm water. After she had put on her robe, their grandmother carefully poured in another pot of boiling water. A sigh of satisfaction came from Hannah. She wriggled down the tub until only her head was above the water. Their grandmother continued her story. "One day, a young man, about 22, arrived at my parents' house with his mother. She was old and dressed in black and looked more like a raisin than a person. They went into the good room with my *bábu* and chatted for over an hour. My *mame* would come out now and then to get some coffee or sweets. I would ask what was happening in the room, and my *mame* would only nod and dash back in. Finally, my *bábu* called me in. I had been waiting in the kitchen. I was supposed to be washing the rice for dinner, but never did; I was too curious about what was going on in the good room."

"*Nána* Hannah, will I get a turn in the bath, or will it be cold?" interrupted Dora.

"Dora, hush! I want to hear the story," hissed Hannah.

"Dora's right, dear. She needs to be clean before your parents come home. Let me scrub you while I talk," and so their grandmother made peace and continued, "I went into the room and there was this wrinkled woman and a tall, handsome man.

"Come here, Hannah my child, " my *bábu* said. 'I want you to meet David. He will be your husband.' I barely heard what he was saying. I was terrified. 'He is a grocer in town and you will marry next year. Say "hello." You do not want him to think you are dumb or stupid.'

So I said hello. My hands were shaking and my body sweating. I thought I would melt into the ground. But he was very kind and had me sit on the chair opposite the couch where he and his mother were sitting. He chatted about his store and his home; I have no idea what he said. Then his mother said something about needing to get back and they left.

"Now, Hannah, out you go. Time for Dora to have a wash," their grandmother said.

Hannah begrudgingly got out of the tub. She quickly covered herself in her robe and then wrapped her hair in a towel. Dora climbed into the tub and shivered. The water wasn't even warm. Their grandmother poured in another pot of boiling water and Dora stretched out. She started scrubbing Dora's back and continued her story, "Right after they left, my *mame* took out my *baoul* and looked inside it. She was disappointed at how little I had. I protested that I was 13 years old, but she was angry. All there was were some embroidered pillowcases and some pillows.

"How I have neglected you," she cried. 'Tonight, we will send your brothers out to invite my sisters and their daughters and your father's sisters and their daughters to come tomorrow and finish this. We have only one year and almost nothing in your *baoul.*'

Now Dora, we must put everything away." The girls cried out for more. "No more stories now, we have to get dressed. Help me drain the tub and move it back behind the stove," commanded their grandmother. Dora climbed out of the tub and stood by the stove as she dried herself. As she dried, Hannah and *Nána* Hannah began emptying the tub by dipping large pots in the tub and dumping them out the window.

Suddenly the door flung open. There stood Alejandro.

"Shut the door," yelled Dora, "you are letting the cold in." He shut the door. "And the world does not need to see me in my bathrobe."

"Where have you been?" asked their grandmother as she stretched her back. He simply shrugged. "Dora, Hannah, get dressed. I will wash Alejandro," ordered their grandmother. The girls did as they were told, they had no desire to help. Their *Shabbat* clothes were the dresses they had received for Rosh Hashanah. Hannah had begged for a traditional outfit like their mother's, and their mother had promised her one when she married. They heard splashing and arguing in the kitchen as their grandmother tried to clean Alejandro.

"Hannah, Dora, come empty the tub," called their grandmother. "Put your robes on to stay dry." And their grandmother disappeared into her room to get dressed. Hannah did as she was asked and Dora did, as well. As they left their room, Alejandro dashed in shivering in his towel. The girls finished emptying the tub, then put it away. Just as Hannah took out a mop to clean the floor, their parents opened the door.

V

Tired, but happy, Miriam and Moses entered their home. Their day had been long in the store, but the stop at the baths had been restoring. They opened the door and smiled to see their daughters being so helpful. Dora was just removing her robe and Hannah was about to mop up some small puddles on the floor. When the girls saw their mother, they dropped their things and ran to her. Miriam gathered her daughters in her arms and savored the moment. Moses stood quietly by until he got his greeting. First, the girls kissed his hand, then he held his precious daughters in his arms.

The quiet entrance of *Shabbat* was shattered by *Nána* Hannah's entry into the room, "Girls, what are you doing? How come the mop is still out? Dora, what is this rag on the floor? Oh, I have not set the *sofah* yet. Children I am so sorry. You work all day and should come home to a ready table."

Moses laughed a large generous laugh, "Mama, relax. Even if it is *Shabbat*, even a queen can sit at an unset *sofah*."

Nána Hannah's eyes crinkled in joy. More than any other of her sons, Moses reminded her of her husband. Alejandro ran out of the bedroom and leapt into his father's arms. Since the older two boys had left for America, Moses had a special fondness for the youngest. Most customs fell away when it came to last remaining son. For Moses, this one boy held all his hopes for the future of the family in Rhodes.

As Moses and Alejandro sat on the couch sharing their day, the women finished setting the table. Dora lay out the white *Shabbat* tablecloth and smoothed it carefully. *Nána* Hannah set out the plates and the glasses, while Hannah set out the cutlery. Miriam did a final polish of the four candles sticks and then placed them on the *sofah*. With that act, she called her men to the *sofah*.

Alejandro's job was to light the *haminero* before his mother lit the *Shabbat* candles. He went to the bench where it was waiting and began his favorite job of putting the kerosene burner inside the large kerosene can. This small cook stove created his favorite *Shabbat* treat: *huevos haminados*.

Once he lit the burner, he would place the pan of salted water, eggs, onion skins, vinegar, and olive oil on the burner. In the morning, he would feast.

As Moses came, he collected a bottle of wine. *Nána* Hannah and Miriam lit their candles, covered their eyes, and recited the blessing in unison. They had done this so long together that the act was almost as if one person were doing it.

Without pausing, although they both had a tear in their eye, they both repeated a prayer for David and Hiam, "*Habarim Buenos...di los alishados.*" ("and good news from far away.")

The children and Moses responded, "*Besorot Tovot.*" ("good news.") It saddened Dora to see the pain her parents felt. As proud as they were of David and Hiam, they knew they'd never see their oldest sons again. The money the brothers sent was much needed and had they stayed on Rhodes their prospects wouldn't have been good. Every day, Dora's parents carried the ache and worry about their oldest two, the joy of their family, and concern for the future in their eyes; Dora saw all of this and so did Hannah, but Alejandro was too young to see. It wasn't as if they were the only family missing someone in America. Almost every Jewish family in the city had sons or fathers overseas sending money home. If they didn't, then they couldn't afford even bread.

Then Moses recited the blessing over the wine and passed the glass around the *sofah*. Next, Moses gathered his three children around him and recited a blessing over them. Then he blessed his wife and mother.

After a quiet moment, *Nána* Hannah took a piece of *reshikas* and said the *motzi*. Slowly, everyone else joined in and ate their bread and salt. Then they finally sat down to dinner.

The salad was already on the *sofah*. Once that was eaten, *Nána* Hannah took the fish with lemon sauce off the stove and placed it on the *sofah*. As Miriam served the family, discussion began.

Alejandro was raising his fork to his mouth when he started the conversation, "*Bábu*, may I invite a friend to dinner during *Hanuka?*"

"Is this child hungry?" asked *Nána* Hannah with much concern. "Do we need to speak to the rabbi about him?"

"No, *Nána* Hannah," Alejandro replied quite seriously.

"Mother," interjected Moses sharply redefining his place as head of the household, "let me get the story. Now, my child, who is this boy and why do we need to invite him?"

"It is my friend, Antonio," answered Alejandro.

"Antonio...Antonio...that is no Jewish name, not a Greek name," pondered his father. "Oh, but you have mentioned his name. His father is one the Italian officials."

"Yes, *Bábu*. Antonio and I play tag and ball on the beach," Alejandro offered helpfully.

"And why does this boy want to visit us? And, more importantly, why do you want this boy to come here?" asked the father.

Alejandro finished a bite of fish, "Well *Bábu*, he invited me for Christmas and it seemed only fair to invite him for Hanukah."

Dora stopped her fork halfway to her mouth. Hannah spilt her glass of water. Miriam dropped her folk on the floor. *Nána* Hannah looked down at her plate. Each awaited the wrath they knew would come.

Moses took a long, slow breath, "I forbid you to go to that home to celebrate a blasphemous holiday! You may not eat in that house. You may not visit that house. Do you hear me?" Slowly as he spoke, his voice grew louder and colder.

"Son," pleaded his mother. "It is *Shabbat*, be peaceful."

Alejandro looked at his father with disbelief, "What is it?"

"Alejandro," responded his father rather severely, "you may not eat in a non-kosher home. I will not have you celebrate a holiday concerned with a person Jews have been accused of murdering for countless generations."

"But *Bábu*," pleaded Alejandro.

"However," and now his voice was gentler, "Antonio is welcome anytime at our home. He is a friend of yours and his people, the Italians, have been generous to us. I see no reason that he cannot discover the truth about us."

Alejandro smiled widely. He jumped out of his chair and embraced his father. The others sprang into movement now that peace had been restored. Dora ate her forkful of fish. Hannah left the *sofah* for a towel to mop up her spill. Their mother retrieved her fork, wiped it on her napkin, and began her fish with a satisfied smile on her face. *Nána* Hannah smiled quietly and soaked in the joy of the holy day and the pleasure of having her family around her.

When the fish was completed, Miriam removed the next course from the oven. Immediately, Hannah expressed her disappointment, "*sevoyas reinadas, tomates reinadas,* and rice?! What happened to the *makaron reinda* you promised?"

"Hannah," reprimanded her mother. "Behave! That is no way to treat your grandmother. She works very hard to take care of us."

"My dear," began her grandmother. "As I was preparing the *makaron* a woman came round begging for food for *Shabbat.* How could I refuse her when we have enough? So I gave what I had handy."

"But *Nána* Hannah, you promised this *Shabbat*..." began Hannah's cry.

Moses jumped in the conversation, "Remember, do a good turn and someday you will be rewarded."

"Also remember," pointed out Miriam, "some are born with good luck, others are destined with bad. Besides you should be satisfied with whatever you have."

Hannah rolled her eyes as she was bombarded with these proverbs. Without a word, she took a *tomate reindas* from the tray as Dora passed it to her. Hannah was quiet through the rest of the meal.

When everyone was done, Dora and Hannah began to clean the *sofah.*

As Hannah reached for the first dish to dry her mother reminded her, "Be careful with those. They were a gift from my brothers."

"Yes, *Mame,*" was Hannah's bored response. "You tell me that every week and every week I am careful." And with exaggerated caution, she stacked the dishes in the sink. She and Dora would wash them after *Havdalah.*

Their grandmother laughed quietly as she brought the fruit and small plates to the *sofah.* Then she took a *ginevra* of coffee and brought that to the *sofah.* Since there was no cooking on *Shabbat, Nána* Hannah had prepared the coffee in the morning and stored it in the *ginevra* to keep it warm. Then they all sat at the *sofah* and listened to Alejandro finish the story of how he won a game at school that day.

VI

The next morning, Moses and Alejandro went to the synagogue. Miriam and her daughters prepared breakfast. They set the *sofah* and drained the *huevos haminados*. Miriam placed on the *sofah* the *kuashado di spinaka*, her mother-in-law had made yesterday and sent to the public ovens. The Turkish owner, Ali, had just sent it back to them by a *hamale*. When the men returned from morning prayers, the family feasted. *Nána* Hannah was well rested from her morning off, so she cleared the *sofah*.

After breakfast and a short rest, Moses asked the children, who were sitting on Dora and Hannah's bed discussing their morning activities, "Who wishes to go with me to visit your Uncle Yitzak?"

"Oh, *Bábu*," moaned Hannah, "Uncle Yitzak is sick. Who wants to visit sick people? I am going to the park with my friends. Come with us Dora." Dora looked at Hannah longingly and then up at her father.

Moses saw the pleading in her eyes. "You go with your sister, Dora. A young girl should spend some time in the fresh air."

"Can I go too?" Alejandro asked his sisters. They looked pleadingly at their father.

"Son, I think your place is with me today. It is time you start doing some man's business," Moses said firmly. Alejandro looked down at the *sofah* dejectedly, but his sisters looked at their father thankfully. "Besides," continued their father, "you never know who will come to visit. I bet some of your cousins will be there."

"Do you think, Cousin Yitzak will be there?" asked Alejandro brightening.

"One never knows. You will just have to come and see," responded his father mysteriously.

VII

The family gathered again at noon for lunch. In fact, almost every family in the *Juderia* had lunch at this time. Miriam and *Nána* Hannah had spent the morning with their friends and relatives visiting and now had much to say.

Nána Hannah began, "I met my cousin Hannah, you know my mother's niece, and she told me about her son." She was so excited she didn't take time to pause, nevertheless eat. "Her son, the one at Montgomery (Where is Montgomery?) is engaged. Can you imagine? He has gone off to who knows where and found himself a Jewish girl."

"Montgomery is in the state of Alabama," Hannah interjected quietly.

Miriam looked up startled, "How do you know that, Hannah? So much about America."

"My friend Sarah. Her *hermanio* lives there in America, just like my *hermanio*," Hannah replied.

Nána Hannah continued her news without acknowledging the interruption. "She is not one of us. A Jew though. Her parents went to America from Germany. Hannah is just pleased she is Jewish, even though she lights the stove on *Shabbat*. Some bad habits one will learn in a strange and foreign country. So far from the community who knows who you will meet? She hopes they will come and visit. Supposedly, she is a good seamstress. They are hoping to open their own tailor shop." Now that she had dispensed her news, she ate her lunch of bread, feta cheese, olives, olive oil, and what was left of breakfast.

Now Hannah could finish her conversation with her mother, "Sarah says Atlanta is nice. Her *hermanio* and Hiam say. They even meet each other at the synagogue. Her *hermanio* lives in a house with a few of his cousins. A widow owns the house and cooks for them. She is Jewish from Germany, keeps kosher and everything. He has a good job in a factory. Sarah wants me to go with her there when she leaves to live with her *hermanio*." Only then, when the story was completely out did Hannah realize she'd said too much.

Her grandmother began to weep, "How can you leave me? I have lost my *inyetos* and now my *ineita*? How can you bring me sadness on this holy day?"

Moses took his mother's hand and turned to Hannah. She cowered in her chair.

His voice sounded like a distant storm: "Do Sarah's parents know of this plan?"

Hannah's voice was almost a squeak: "They told Sarah they are saving to send her. She is engaged to a cousin who is there with her *hermanio*. She has four brothers and two sisters younger than her. They need the money."

"They may do as they please; Sarah is their daughter," commented Moses coldly. "You, however, are my daughter. So long as you are my responsibility, you may not go. And you can be assured I shall make no match for you, or Dora, with a man who plans to leave the island. I could not stop your brothers; they were men when they made their decision. However, you are only girls and no more of my children are leaving the family."

Then he turned to his mother to comfort her. "Come, Mama, it is time to nap." And he led her from the *sofah*.

VIII

By the time Moses had fixed his clothes and taken out the cups, his father-in-law Hiam had arrived with his brother, David. Slowly, a few cousins arrived. They gathered around and started discussing the *parsha* while drinking their black bitter Turkish coffee.

Hannah got up and dressed.

"Where are you going?" asked Dora.

"To Sarah's to play cards," Hannah replied.

Dora yawned, "How dull." Then she turned over and returned to her book. Hannah quietly shut the door behind her.

"Bye *Bábu*," she called as she left.

"Hannah, do you have a hug for your *nóno*?" called out Hiam. Hannah ran back in to share a hug.

"Where are you off to, child?" asked her father.

"To Sarah's to play cards."

"Enjoy, be home between *minha* and *avrit*," reminded her father and the men returned to their discussion.

After some time, Miriam awoke and got dressed. She interrupted the men only long enough to greet them and find two cups. After pouring the coffee from the *ginevra*, she took the cups to her mother-in-law's room on a tray along with two glasses of water, as well. At least once a week she felt she should treat her mother-in-law to coffee in bed.

"Are the men deep in discussion?" asked Hannah as she sat up and took her coffee.

Miriam set the tray on a small table.

"Yes," she replied settling into the chair. "Their afternoon *kaveh* is heated. It just is not the same as when we were first married."

"No, it is not," Hannah answered. "There are so few men these days."

Miriam smiled a small smile and leaned back.

"Do you miss their arguments?" she asked.

"You are kind, daughter," laughed Hannah. "Remember table pounding and a broken cup or two?"

Miriam giggled, her shoulders shaking, "My *hermanio* was famous for his temper. I never thought I would miss gluing those cups back together." Her voice turned sad, "I wonder when he will send another letter. His child must be born. How can you raise a child so far from their family? How will they know their namesake? I wonder if it is a Dora or a Hiam."

Hannah put down her cup.

"It will be fine. That little Dora or Hiam will be raised in a *Rhodelisi* home, even if they are not here, but are some place called the Congo."

"I know, I know," Miriam replied. "Anyway, I should make sure the men get to *minha* so we can prepare for *havdalah*." Miriam sighed deeply and rose heavily. She took the tray, kissed Hannah on the forehead, and left the room.

Hannah lay back in her bed savoring a few more moments of rest. Every *Shabbat* she realized how precious this rest was and how much more difficult every week was becoming. Then she smiled as she heard her daughter-in-law gently persuade the men it was time for them to get to synagogue. She closed her eyes and fell asleep again.

Miriam gathered the dirty empty cups and put them in the sink. She put the white *Shabbat* table cloth back on the *sofah*. Luckily, there were only a few wine stains from the previous night. Then she took the *havdalah* set out of the cabinet. Dora came into the room.

Without looking up, Miriam said, "Dora, we must remember to buy a new *havdalah* candle this week."

"I'll try, *mame*," answered a sleepy voice.

"Dora," Miriam began and then looked up. "Oh child of mine, please go brush your hair," she said laughing.

"Yes, *mame*," the girl replied.

Miriam shook her head as she found the bottle of wine. Now that the *sofah* was ready, Miriam sat down and picked up the letters from her brother. She kept them, and the ones from her sons, in a box and took them out every *Shabbat* to reread. She hummed as she worked. Dora came in and sat beside her mother. Her dress was clean and her hair brushed. She started humming with her mother and then broke into song.

En la mar ay una torre	In the sea there is a tower
En la torre ay una ventana	In the tower there is a window
I en las ventana, ay una ninya	And in the window there is a young maiden
Ke a los marieneros yama	Who calls the sailors to her
I en la ventana ay una ninay	And in the window there is a young maiden
Ke a los marieneros yama	Who calls the sailors to her
Si la mar era de leche	If the sea were made of milk
I los barkitos de kanela	And the rowboats made of cinnamon
Yo me mancharia intera por	I would dive in
Delivrar la mi bandiera	To rescue my country's flag
Yo me mancharia intera por	I would dive in
Delivrar la mi bandiera.	To rescue my country's flag.
No me yeves tu al mueye	Do not take me to the pier
A los doz de la manyana	At two in the morning
A la luz de la farola	Because there is the light from the lighthouse
Todo el mundo me konose	And all the world will recognize me
A la luz de la farola	Because there is the light from the lighthouse
Todo el mundo me konose.	And all the world will recognize me.

When they finished their music, Miriam kissed her daughter's forehead. They smiled at each other and rested in the glow of the song.

Then Hannah came running into the house laughing, "I won! I won!"

"Well, *mazal tov*," her mother grinned. "And how much did you win?" Hannah handed her a small bag filled with almonds. "Well, you had some good cards. What did you girls talk about?" Hannah smiled and clenched her lips together. Then she winked at Dora and spun around to face the door she had just entered.

Looking over her shoulder at her mother, she said, as innocently as she could, "Oh, nothing, *mame*." And she hurried to her room. Miriam smiled to herself and nodded knowingly.

"*Mame*," said Dora quickly. "I really must go do *something* in my room." And she extricated herself from her mother's arms and dashed the room she shared with Hannah and Alejandro.

Miriam laughed out loud and said to no one but herself, "I wonder what Sarah and Hannah were talking about." And shaking her head in memory of her *Shabbat* afternoons playing cards and gossiping with friends, she resumed her reading.

IX

Dora dashed into the room she shared with her brother and sister and shut the door behind her. There lay Hannah sprawled on the bed with her feet on the floor staring at the ceiling.

"What happened at Sarah's? Quick, tell me!" begged Dora as she climbed on to the end of the bed. Hannah just kept staring at the ceiling. Dora, kneeling on the bed, put her hands by her knees and leaned over her sister's face, assuring that there was no way Hannah could avoid looking at her. "Hannah. Oh, Hannah. Come back from Mount Sinai, older sister, and tell me the news."

"News?" asked Hannah innocently as she turned to face her little sister.

"Oh please," groaned Dora. "I know you know something. Tell me! Tell me!!"

Hannah sat up slowly and asked quietly, "What gave you the idea I have any news?" And she studied her hands, contemplating her broken nails.

Dora started to playfully pound Hannah with her fists, "Stop it! You're just teasing me!"

With that, Hannah pulled her feet up under her, looked into her sister's almond-shaped brown eyes, and said almost as one word, "Sarah-got-a-letter-from-her betrothed."

Dora's jaw dropped, "And so? Why is this exciting?

"Welllllll," began Hannah, "he not only talked about his work in the factory and Sarah's *hermanio* and the German Jewish blue-eyed lady who runs the boarding house…"

"What?!" Dora exclaimed horrified. "They live in a house owned by someone with blue-eyes? Their lives must be filled with bad luck. What are they doing to guard against the evil eye?"

"Silly girl," retorted Hannah. "You're just superstitious. We do live in the modern era, you know. Anyway, he sent her a love poem."

Dora's eyes grew large, "A love poem? Did you see it? Was it beautiful?"

"Oh, it was wonderful. How could it not be?" Hannah's voice softened at the memory of the poem. "He should have gone to university and become a teacher. He described himself as her slave of love..."

"Just like in the song *Esklava de amor*," sighed Dora.

"And described their lives like in the song '*Siente Joya el Son de Mi Gitara*.' Then he compared the mailman to a dove because he carries their letter and love across the sea."

Dora fell back on the bed, "How romantic. How sad they are apart." Hannah fell back as well and sighed. There they lay for quite some time until their father and brother returned from the *avrit* service.

X

After the *avrit* service, when Moses entered his home holding the hand of his remaining son, he took a deep breath. This was the moment he savored the most; the house, in fact the entire *Juderia*, was quiet with the special rest of *Shabbat*. Once he called everyone to the table, the ease of this holy day would disappear as they performed the ancient observance of *havdalah*.

Blowing out his breath quite loudly, Moses called out, "Come, everyone. It is time kiss the *Shabbat* Bride good-bye."

Miriam rose from the couch she had been reading on and walked up behind her husband. She gently put her right hand on his left shoulder. He turned his head to look at her. They were the same height, something he enjoyed because they looked at each other in the eye; as he teased her often, they had to see eye-to-eye, thus, their disagreements were always resolved. How he loved those beautiful almond-shaped brown eyes. They spoke to him the secrets of his beloved's heart. What could he do but smile? Dora and Hannah came out of their room, smoothing their dresses. The family gathered around the table. Moses was about to light the *havdalah* candle when he stopped in mid-match strike.

"Where is *Nána* Hannah?" he inquired with some concern.

Alejandro jumped at the opportunity to be helpful, "I will go get her."

"No!" commanded his father. Two concerns crossed his mind. First, what if something really was wrong with his mother, would he want his seven-year-old son to discover this? Absolutely not. Second, what if she was undressed or dressing. It would be improper for his son to see a woman in a state of undress. He put his hand on his son's shoulder, "You are kind to offer. However, I think it would be more proper if your mother went to get *Nána*." And he looked at his wife, raised one eyebrow, and nodded at her very slightly.

She returned the nod and went to her mother-in-law's room. She knocked on the door frame. There was no answer. Now, she too was concerned.

She knocked again and called out softly, "*Esfuegra*, are you alright?" Still there was no answer. So Miriam went in. There was her mother-in-law sleeping on the bed. Miriam walked quietly over to the bedside and laid her hand on Hannah's arm. Gently, she shook the arm. "Mama, wake up. It is time for *havdalah*." Hannah finally opened her eyes.

"Is it so late already," she asked. "I simply lay back down and closed my eyes for only a moment."

"It is 'that late'," Miriam said with a smile. "Come, I will help you get dressed and we will go enjoy *havdalah*." And Miriam offered her hand to Hannah to help her sit up. Hannah sat up and her eyes popped open and then she swayed in the bed.

"I do not feel so well, daughter," she said.

"Your hand is hot. Are you dizzy?"

"Am I hot? I cannot tell, but the room will not sit still," responded Hannah.

"Lay back down," commanded her daughter-in-law. "I will get you a cloth for your head." And she lovingly tucked Hannah back into bed and left the room. From the kitchen, she took a clean cloth and dunked it in the cistern outside the kitchen door. Before she brought it into the house, she wrung it out. Then she went back to Hannah's room and laid the cool damp cloth on the old woman's head. Hannah had already fallen asleep again. Now, Miriam went back to her family.

Moses looked at his wife expectantly, "Where is my mother?"

"She is not feeling very well. I do not think it is anything major. We should send Dora for La Prima after *havdalah*." Miriam suggested quietly.

Moses pondered this for a moment and then realized that his wife was almost always correct about such things. So he lit the four wicks on the *havdalah* candle and handed the candle to Alejandro.

Next, he poured a cup of wine and recited the traditional blessing over wine: "*Baruch atah adonoy elohanu melech ha-ohlam, boray p'ree hagafen.*" (Blessed are you, Lord our G-d, Ruler of the universe, Creator of the fruit of the vine.) Then Moses lifted the spice box and recited the blessing: "*Baruch atah adonoy elohanu melech ha-ohlam, boray ha-aretz.*" (Blessed are you, Lord our G-d, Ruler of the universe, Creator of the fruit of the tree.) This small, footed, silver box was passed around the table so that each person could hold it to their nose and smell the tangy scent of lemon rind through the tiny holes punched in an elegant pattern around the box and savor the *Shabbat* smells. When the box was returned to the table, Moses took the candle from Alejandro and recited the blessing for the candle: "*Baruch atah adonoy elohanu melech ha-ohlam, boray m'ohray ha-aysh.*" (Blessed are you, Lord our G-d, Ruler of the universe, Creator of the light of fire.) Moses paused for a moment before he recited the final blessing of the ceremony because he wanted to hold onto the wonders of *Shabbat* for one final moment. He took a breath and recited the blessing that closes *Shabbat:* "*Baruch atah adonoy elohanu melech ha-ohlam, hamav'deel bayn kodesh l'chol, bayn or l'ch'shech, bayn yom hash'vee-ee l'shayshet y'may hama'aseh. Baruch atah adonoy hamav'deel bayn kodesh l'chol.*" (Blessed are you, Lord our G-d, Ruler of the universe, who separates sacred from profane, light from darkness, the seventh day of rest from the six days of labor. Blessed is the Lord, who separates the sacred from the profane.) After taking a sip of wine from the cup, he handed the cup to his wife, who took her sip and passed it to Hannah. The cup made the entire circle of the family and was returned to Moses. Then he doused the candle's flames in the little wine that was left by tilting the cup sliding the candle, flames first, into it. The entire family could hear the sputter as the sacred flames were extinguished. Then they sang their wish for the Elijah the Prophet to come soon to foretell the arrival of the Messiah.

As soon as they had finished singing, Dora looked at her mother. Miriam gave her a quick nod and Dora dashed out into the street to find La Prima, a noted healer. Dora believed that she must be at her home since everyone was just finishing the *havdalah* ceremony. It was at her home where Dora found her.

"Please, La Prima, we need you! My *nána* is ill and my *mame* Miriam asks you to hurry," Dora begged.

"Your *nána? En Koyamar.* I will come," and with that statement the elderly woman rose regally from her chair. Dressed in her traditional clothes, she practically glided down the cobble street behind Dora. It seemed to people that she really didn't walk; La Prima was too fine a woman for that.

When they arrived back at Dora's home, Dora shouted out, "I have her!"

Miriam raised her left hand to her forehead and shook her head.

"Dora, Dora, my child, that is no way to enter this home and that is no way to introduce a guest, especially one as important as this one," commented Miriam. Then she turned to La Prima and welcomed her properly, "Thank you for coming to our home and seeing to my *esfuegra* Hannah."

La Prima looked passed Miriam and without responding to the greeting, demanded, *"Traimi un punado de sal!"* (Bring me a fistful of salt!) Had Miriam not known this woman since she was born, she would have thought her rude. Instead, Miriam had expected this demand and produced a fistful of salt she had held in her right hand. She held La Prima's hand in her left hand as she loosened her fist and poured the salt into the older woman's hand. *"Kualo es esto?"* (What is this?), demanded La Prima.

Miriam answered with the single word, *"sal."* Dora watched this ceremony without saying a word. She, too, had grown up with it. Then Miriam led La Prima to Hannah's room.

Then La Prima chanted about the salt and how it would dissolve in the sea and take the illness with it. The healer called upon G-d, Abraham, Isaac, Jacob, and Moses, among others. She sang about meeting with Elijah the Prophet and telling him about Hannah. Then La Prima began the chant that she repeated seven times. During this chant she yawned, trying to get Hannah to awaken and yawn with her to force out any bad gases in Hannah's system and she circled Hannah's upper body, arms, and head with her fist.

Miriam returned to Hannah's bedroom with a pitcher of water and a bowl. Miriam placed the bowl on the table and poured in the water. La Prima then tossed the salt into the bowl. Gently, she stirred the water and salt and then began rubbing it on Hannah's face, arms and legs. Moses, who had come to sit with his mother as soon as the *havdalah* ceremony was concluded, turned his head away when La Prima lifted the covers to expose Hannah's legs. He felt it improper to see his mother's legs.

Finally, La Prima Sara de Bohor Notrica carried the bowl to the window, threw the salt water out, and chanted, "*El Dio ke lo guadre de todo modo de mal.*" ("May G-d keep him from all evil.")

With the ceremony done, La Prima wished everyone a good week and Dora escorted her to the door.

Nána Hannah signed deeply and asked in a small voice, "May I have a cup of tea?"

"Of course, *Mame*," Moses replied and shooed everyone out of his mother's bedroom.

Miriam lit the stove, now that it was no longer *Shabbat*, and set the kettle to boil. While she waited, she gathered the ingredients for the tea: *tilia*, cinnamon, and lemon. She put the items in the teapot and poured in the boiling water. Then Miriam put a miniature sieve over the cup and poured the water over it. The sieve caught the spices. The tea smelled amazing. Miriam put the cup on a saucer and placed them on a tray. Carefully, she carried the tray into her mother-in-law's room.

"Hannah? Hannah? Are you still awake?" whispered Miriam.

"Hnnn," came the muffled reply. Miriam entered the darkened room and set the tray on the side table. Hannah turned over and tried to sit up.

"Mother, let me put some pillows behind you," Miriam said gently and took the cushions off the chair to put behind Hannah. Then she helped her mother-in-law drink her tea.

"*Gracias*, Miriam," Hannah mumbled. "I feel better already." And Hannah fell asleep propped in her bed.

Miriam smiled and shut the door behind her as she left.

XI

A few weeks later Alejandro reminded his father of the promise he had made, "*Bábu*, what night of *Hanukah* should I invite Antonio home?"

Moses' hand stopped halfway to his mouth and with a weak sigh he put the glass back down on the dinner table. He had forgotten about his promise that the Italian boy could come. He looked at Miriam for assistance. She smiled mischievously and shrugged her shoulders. There was no way out of this now. Moses' mother had a sudden coughing fit that she hid in her napkin.

Moses cleared his throat, "Well, how about tomorrow – the first night?"

Alejandro bit the left side of his lower lip while he thought, "Well...it is not much notice. If that is not good, will the second night be good?"

"Ask your *nána*," Moses replied gruffly. "I do not do the cooking." His mother held back a grin, so he was passing the responsibility off on her. Some children never grow up.

"*Nána?*" was Alejandro's simple question.

"*Inieto*," his grandmother said, "there is always enough food for one more. Bring Antonio when it suits you both." That answer suited Alejandro quite nicely.

XII

The next evening after dinner, Moses took the *hanukiah* off the shelf and placed it on the table. Then he poured oil in two of the cups and placed the wicks in them, and finally he called his family.

"Come, time to light the Hanukah lights!"

Everyone stood round the *sofah*, but *Nána* Hannah sat. Since her illness, she often sat more.

Moses recited the blessings: "*Baruch atah Adoni elohanu melech ho-aolam, asher kid shanu b'mitzvohtav, v'tzivanu l'had'lik nair shel Chanukah. Baruch atah Adoni elohanu melech ho-aolam, she'ahsah nisim la-ahvotaynu bayamim ha haym hazman hazeh. Baruch atah Adoni elohanu melech ho-aolam, she hecheyanu v'ki-imanu v'higi-anu lazman hazeh.*" (Blessed are you, oh Lord our G-d, Ruler of the universe, who commanded us to kindle the light of *Hanukah*. Blessed are you, oh Lord our G-d, Ruler of the universe, Who performed miracles for our ancestors in those days at this time. Blessed are you, oh Lord our G-d, Ruler of the universe, who has brought us to this season to celebrate.)

Everyone responded, "Amen."

Then *Nána* Hannah brought out a tray of *burmuelos*. She had begun these before dinner by mixing the dough and putting it aside to rise. After dinner, as her son cleaned the *hanukia*, she quickly heated the oil, shaped little dough balls, and fried them. Now she came to the *sofah* with the hot fritters drizzled with honey. Miriam appeared with coffee and everyone feasted on this *Hanukah* treat.

The next day, Monday, in the courtyard of the school as Alejandro and Antonio met on their way into class, Alejandro turned to his friend an asked in Italian, "Can you come over for *Hanukah* tonight?"

"Tonight?" repeated Antonio. "I do not know."

"If not tonight, then tomorrow," Alejandro responded in a hush as they entered the building to begin their school day. They had no chance to talk again because once school was over Alejandro was whisked away by his sisters and Antonito's mother met him at the gate.

XIII

As the girls were clearing the dinner table, there was a light knock at the door. Alejandro looked up expectantly and Moses was shocked. He didn't think they were expecting anyone. However, a knock at the door should be answered, so Moses rose from the table. As he passed his wife's chair, he put a hand gently on her shoulder. Moses opened the door to find a well-dressed 8-year-old boy whom he didn't know looking at him expectantly. Moses looked severely down at this black-haired olive-skinned child who looked up at him with large brown eyes as if they knew each other.

Their silence was broken by Miriam who called out, "My *espozo*, who do you keep at the door for so long?" Moses realized he didn't have an answer. Suddenly, or so it seemed to him, Alejandro was standing beside him bounding up and down, pulling on his sleeve.

"I told you, *Bábu*! I told you!" he squealed excitedly.

"What?"

"That Antonio would come," was the quick response as Alejandro took his friend's hand and led him around his father. The boys marched together to the table where Moses watched Alejandro in a child's unconscious mimicry of adults introduce his mother to his Christian friend. Moses then shut the front door and took the *hanukiah* off the shelf and placed it on the table. Alejandro had already given Antonio his chair and was returning with one from another room. Dora and Hannah took their seats without taking real notice of the guest. All four children watched Moses fill three cups with oil and add a wick to each.

"What is this?" asked Antonio in a whisper.

"A *hanukiah*," replied Alejandro in his usual voice.

"What is it for? These three small wicks will certainly not light this room," asked the Italian boy in a hush.

Alejandro looked at his friend with surprise, "Do not have one at your house?" Dora started to giggle until Hannah kicked her under the *sofah*. They knew the Christians didn't celebrate Hanukah, but this was Alejandro's first Christian friend. Antonio gave his friend a curious look and shook his head violently. Moses began to open his mouth and answer until he saw the slightest shake of his wife's head. Before the conversation could continue, the matriarch returned.

"Who is this?" she inquired with the sparkle in her eye reserved for all children.

"*Nána* Hannah, this is my friend Antonio," answered her grandson.

Antonio pulled on his sleeve and whispered, "What are you saying?" Alejandro didn't realize that he was speaking in two different languages: Italian to his friend and *Ladino* to his grandmother.

He switched, consciously, to Italian and continued with his grandmother, "You said I could bring him tonight." His grandmother looked at him blankly.

"Speak to your *nána* in *maestro espaniol*," commanded Moses curtly to his son.

Alejandro hung his head at the reprimand in front of his friend and said humbly in *Ladino*, "You said I could bring him tonight."

His grandmother responded as if nothing had happened, "Of course, and welcome to our house, our friend."

The conversation hadn't interrupted Antonio's curiosity.

He pulled on his friend's sleeve and whispered again, "What are those lamps for?"

"Well," began Alejandro with a puff of his chest. He felt very much like their beloved teacher. Everyone sat expectantly to see if he gave the correct answer, "see the one that looks like a teapot?" Antonio nodded. "That's called the *shamash*. We use it to light the other wicks so that no wick is jealous of any other that it got lit by the match." And so Alejandro felt he had concluded the discussion and sat down. Miriam suppressed a smile; she knew what was coming.

Antonio was still confused, "But *why* do you light these lamps?" Now, he was no longer whispering.

"Because it is *Hanukah*," was Alejandro's quick curt reply with a confused look on his face. It did not occur to him that his Christian friend had no idea what the story of the festival was.

"But *what* is *Hanukah*?!" was Antonio's exasperated request with a bang of his fist on the *sofah*. Even Moses had to smile at this adult mannerism.

"Oh, that. When King Antiochus of Syria tried to make the Jews in the Holy Land to be less Jewish, the Jews fought back. You do know that this was before the year zero – over 200 years before? Our leader was Judah Maccabee and he led the Jews in great battles and won. After the fighting, the Jews went to the Temple in Jerusalem and found it destroyed with pigs inside. They scrubbed and fixed and then went to light the eternal flame, but there was only one small container of oil for the lamp." Antonio was transfixed by the story; he hadn't taken his eyes off of Alejandro this whole time. "They decided to light the lamp and send someone to the place where the oil was made, even though they knew that the oil would not last the full eight days it would take for someone to get there and back. But a miracle happened. The little jar of oil lasted the entire time. And that is why we celebrate the festival for eight days."

There was a collective sigh around the *sofah* and everyone smiled. Moses and Miriam exchanged smiles. Their son had retold the story very well, with accuracy. Antonio sat quietly and then said, "Thank you for telling such an interesting story."

Moses took out the box of matches and lit the "teapot," as Alejandro had called it and recited the blessings: "*Baruch atah Adoni elohanu melech ho-aolam, asher kid shanu b'mitzvohtav, v'tzivanu l'had'lik nair shel Chanukah. Baruch atah Adoni elohanu melech ho-aolam, she'ahsah nisim la-ahvotaynu bayamim ha haym hazman hazeh.*" (Blessed are you, oh Lord our G-d, Ruler of the universe, who commanded us to kindle the light of *Hanukah*. Blessed are you, oh Lord our G-d, Ruler of the universe, who performed miracles for our ancestors in those days at this time.)

Everyone responded, "Amen."

Nána Hannah pushed back her chair with a loud scrape on the floor and went into the kitchen with the sound of her *patuklas* following her. She came back with a tray of fresh *bumeulos*.

"What are these?" Antonio asked in Italian. Now he was not whispering because he realized that no one would make fun of his ignorance.

"*Bumeulos*," answered Dora. "We eat them for *Hanukah*."

"Why?"

36

"Yes, why do we eat them?" asked Alejandro as he stuffed one in his mouth.

Hannah took this opportunity, "Because they are fried in oil, they remind us of the oil to keep the eternal light lit."

"*Grazie*," responded Antonio as he shoved another *bumeulo* into his mouth. When they had finished eating, Antonio announced he should leave as it was late.

Miriam declared, "You cannot walk home alone at this hour. Alejandro, why not you walk him home and take your sisters with you?" The boys practically leapt out of their seats and then Antonio remembered his manners.

He turned to Miriam, gave a slight bow, and said, "*Grazie*." Then he strode over to Moses and shook his hand. As he walked over to his friend's grandmother, he chewed on the very tip of his left thumb unsure of how to thank this woman with whom he shared no common language, for such fine treats. She saw the uncertainty in his eyes and gave him her most gracious grandmotherly smile. He burst into a big grin and gave her a big hug as she sat in her chair. Then he skipped back to his friend and grabbed his hand. Hannah and Dora excused themselves and the four children left the house for a pleasant night's stroll.

XIV

On Wednesday evening, the fourth night of *Hanukah*, *Nána* Dora and *Nóno* Hiam, and *Tiya* Alejandra and *Tiyo* Noah joined the family for dinner. The children loved their aunt and uncle very much. The two in their early 30s, had been married a number of years, but as yet had no children; thus, Miriam's five children were favorites of theirs.

Tonight, after dinner and *bumeulos*, *Nóno* Hiam called on each child in turn, "Hannah, what have you learned this week in school?"

Hannah smiled and responded, "I have learned how to conjugate an irregular verb in French."

Her grandfather stroked his beard, "Was this hard?"

"For some, but not for me!" was his *ineita*'s quick reply.

"Good. And you, little Dora?" Only he and *Nána* Dora referred to her this way. Hiam argued how else he could tell his wife from her namesake, their *ineita*.

Dora knew this request was coming and had prepared all day, "I have been learning multiplication in three and four digits." Her grandparents smiled.

"Now, *inieto*, what have you learned?" asked this proud grandfather of his youngest grandchild.

"Well, *Nóno* I learned something very important, but not at school."

"Have you learned nothing at school this week?"

"Oh, *Nóno* I have," quickly responded Alejandro. These children had learned quickly how important their schooling was to their parents and grandparents. "But I think this is even more interesting."

His grandfather leaned forward with much interest and said most seriously, "Then you must tell me."

Alejandro leaned in, as did everyone around the *sofah* to hear this interesting tidbit, and said in his most serious and adult voice with a tone that implied this was some amazing secret, "Did you know, *Nóno*, that Christians do not know what *Hanukah* is and do not have *hannukiah* in their homes?" His grandfather leaned back in his chair and gave a big belly laugh. Then he reached out to his littlest grandchild and gave him a bear hug.

"You are right, that is perhaps the most important lesson you can learn." Everyone laughed with the patriarch. "Now children, a small gift for learning such important lessons." The three filed around the *sofah* and received change from their grandfather, uncle, and father.

"Now," began their father, "just because you can treat yourselves to a day free from school tomorrow, does not mean you can forgo your studies. I expect each of you to spend some time reading tomorrow."

"Yes, *Bápu*," came the unison chorus of voices who had not registered anything their father said as they walked to their room. They were busy counting their coins and seeing if they had enough to buy the lunch they had planned on.

With the children busy, the adults sat back with their coffee to chat.

"Miriam, what news of David and Hiam?" asked her brother-in-law Noah.

Miriam could not help herself and let out a deep sigh, "The usual mostly." And she pulled their most recent letters from her blouse. She had started carrying those precious words from her sons near her heart so that she could keep them with her. "David writes about how lucky they are to have work. It seems that some people are having difficulty finding jobs, especially those who do not know good English. But they are well respected with their jobs as shoemakers."

"The boys," the elder Dora smiled, "They have a skill now."

Moses interjected, "They say their English is quite good. The Atlanta Federation of Jewish Charities has classes for the arriving men to study in. David says that Hiam is very good with his reading, as well as his speaking. Unfortunately," and here his voice became sad, "David has given up his studies. He is working extra so that Hiam can study more."

"I am sure that his brother will return the favor in time," offered Alejandra gently.

"They have moved," jumped in Miriam trying to regain the conversation. "Mrs. Amiel did not like the house they were in and found them a more suitable boarding house."

"Oh, I have heard others talk of Mrs. Amiel," commented Alejandra. "Her name is Rebecca. I believe we know her family. If I remember they were always generous. She helps all the newcomers, does she not?"

"Oh yes," replied her sister. "She made sure the boys enrolled with the Atlanta Federation and tried to find them a suitable place to live."

"Blessed by the Lord, they are no longer living with the blue-eyed devil like Sarah's relative," mumbled the elder Hannah. Miriam looked at her crossly; she didn't like the older woman's superstitious ways.

The conversation continued for some time until Hiam turned to his wife and said, "Come, *vos*, you look tired and I am too old to carry you home as you sleep." His wife smiled, winked at her daughters, and rose to go. They all knew that it was really he who was tired, but felt it unmanly to admit to such a thing.

"Well *Bápu*," retorted Alejandra with a wicked gleam in her eye for her mother and sister, "I guess Noah and I should escort you home. We all know that Mama gets easily lost in the maze of the *Juderea*." Miriam smiled, though she dared not laugh. Only her sister could make mention of the time their father had gotten drunk on *Purim* one year and gotten lost on his way home. How he had gotten lost in *Juderia* where he had grown up even he didn't know. Their mother bit her lower lip with the two teeth she had left in her upper gum to keep back the smile. And so the mood was lightened and everyone prepared themselves for bed.

XV

Saturday Moses was about to leave for morning services with Alejandro, Miriam called out, "*El*, wait! Have you forgotten something?"

"What more does a man need for *Shabbat* service than his *tallit* and his son?" asked Moses raising his hands. On one was his *tallit* bag and in the other was his son's hand.

Miriam laughed, "Usually, you would be ready, but today is *Shabbat Halbashah*. You need to take this bundle of clothes as well."

Moses dropped Alejandro's hand and took the bundle from his wife, "How could I forget? *Gracias*." And they were on their way.

"*Bápu*," inquired Alejandro. "Why do we take clothes to the synagogue today?"

"My *fijo*," responded his father gently, "would you be kind enough to carry my *tallit*?" And he handed over the *tallit* bag to Alejandro. "*Gracias*. The clothes we bring go to those less fortunate mostly in the *Juderia*, but to some non-Jews as well. So do not comment to anyone that their clothes look familiar. We are forbidden by Jewish law to shame anyone."

"But, *Bápu, hermanio* sends us money, how can we give away our clothes?" was Alejandro's innocent question.

"*Echa un pedasiko de pan a la mar, algun dia lo toparas* (Do a good turn and someday you will be rewarded) is what my *Bápu* taught me," answered his father. And the conversation ended as they entered the courtyard of the *Kal de Shalom* synagogue. There, in the courtyard, were a number of bundles already to which Moses added theirs.

XVI

Alejandro remembered the last time he had asked his father this question; he was pretty sure this time wasn't going to go any better. Antonio had asked again if Alejandro would come and have Christmas dinner at his house. He tried hard to think of some clever way to convince his father to let him go. He tried hard to come up with some half lie. Neither worked. Alejandro knew his father was too clever to be fooled and didn't believe he could live with himself if he made such a huge lie. So he decided a straight forward approach was his best mode of attack.

Both Dora and Hannah noticed Alejandro was unusually quiet on their way home from school.

"Little beast, why are you so quiet?" asked Hannah. "Usually you chatter more than a parakeet."

There was no response. Dora and Hannah looked at each other in surprise over his head. Usually the nickname "little beast" evoked some response. Hannah gently slapped Dora behind Alejandro's back and cocked her head. Dora chewed on the left corner of her lower lip and smiled, she knew how to get him.

"I heard that little Miriam likes Alejandro. Did you, Hannah?" Dora knew her sister would play along with this.

"Little Miriam, eh? That would make a fine match. I am sure that someday her mouth will grow around those front teeth and a proper *yazma* will cover that untamed hair."

"Unless, of course," added Dora with a twinkle in her eye, "she does actually shave her head. Then we will never know if it gets tamed or not."

Alejandro didn't even notice them. He walked on totally enveloped in his thoughts on how he'll convince his father to let him go to Antonio's for Christmas. The sisters were dumbfounded. They could think of nothing more to say, so the three finished their walk home in silence.

This revelry continued all evening. Alejandro was unusually silent. His parents were terribly concerned, though they said nothing. Alejandro always had something to interject into the conversation; some tidbit ha had learned in school or gossip heard on the street, but today he barely said the

42

"amen" after the Hannukah candles were blessed. Finally, his father could stand it no longer.

"*Fijo*, my last son, what is the problem?" Moses asked gently.

Alejandro looked up at his father with the saddest eyes his father had ever seen and sighed.

"*Bábu*, there is something I desperately wish for and I cannot have. You have forbidden it. There is no point in me asking you, or you asking me." Moses' heart broke. He loved his five children with all his heart. He sacrificed for all of them. He gave up many necessities so that his children could go to school. He wept at night for David and Hiam, but their desire had been to go. He even held off prospective matches for Hannah because he wanted her to finish school and pick a mate. What had he denied his youngest, his last son, that brought him so much pain?

"*Fijo*, come here," Moses begged patting his lap. Alejandro dutifully walked to his father and climbed on his lap. Everyone else watched, holding their breath. Without a doubt Alejandro was spoiled. Being the youngest meant he was pampered and coddled. "Tell me, what do you so desire?"

"*Bábu*, I want to have dinner at Antonio's house," Alejandro replied tearfully.

"And why is this such a problem? If you keep the laws of *kashrut*, there is no problem. Your brothers and sisters have eaten at the houses of Christian friends on occasion," inquired his father.

"Oh yes," jumped in Dora trying to be helpful. "Remember, I had dinner at Maria's two months ago for her birthday a bunch of us girls were there."

Moses smiled at Dora and turned back to Alejandro, "Tell me what this special occasion is."

Alejandro looked at him with pained eyes, cringed, and whispered so softly only his father could hear, "Christmas." Moses tensed. Alejandro could feel it, but now he was ensconced on his father's lap; he couldn't get off. Everyone else looked on expectantly, because they neither heard Alejandro nor felt Moses.

"Alejandro," Moses' tone said it all. He was neither loud nor quiet and every syllable was controlled. Miriam hung her head, waiting for her husband to explode. "I will not. I cannot allow you to celebrate the birth of a false messiah whose followers have persecuted us for nearly 2000 years."

"But *Bábu*," begged Alejandro.

"There are no buts," was the stern and swift reply.

Miriam decided to try her hand at compromise, "Come *El*, perhaps there is a way." Alejandro looked up hopefully. Moses lifted his son off his lap and stood him up, like toy soldier.

"There is *no* way," he retorted.

The anxiety inside Alejandro was too much to bear. He ran from the room crying. *Nána* Hannah looked at her son with a mixture of resignation and disgust and followed her grandson to his room. The girls sat afraid to move.

"Hannah, Dora, go wash the dishes in the kitchen," commanded their mother. They rose and left the room hastily, thankful for the opportunity to leave. Experience had taught them that whatever was to follow was not going to be pleasant and they had no desire to witness it.

Miriam and Moses stared at each other across the *sofah*. The silence was uncomfortable, but neither wanted to break it.

"You broke his heart," began Miriam finally staring at her hands that were folded gently on the table.

"It will heal," responded Moses curtly.

"Did you have too? It is only a meal," retorted Miriam raising her eyes, but not her head. "The others have shared meals with their Christian friends."

"*Not* Christmas," he grunted in return.

"He does not understand."

"He will understand more if he experiences it."

"What if they try to convert him?"

"Ah, now we get to the heart of the matter," came Miriam's reply with a grin. She sat back in her chair, more at ease. "Do you really think they could do that in one meal?"

"Well,…" Moses sounded less assured.

"Oh Moses, you can be so silly sometimes. The worst thing that can happen to the boy is that he will eat from an un*kosher* kitchen. He is not even the type to eat *traife* food. Let him go," Miriam said rolling her eyes.

"I cannot. I have said 'No.' *De la kavesa, fiede el pishkado* (The head of the family determines the outcome of the family)," Moses replied with much bravado and a bang of his hand on the table.

"So I have convinced you, but you are now afraid to lose face. Why did I ever let my parents convince me to marry you?" and Miriam sighed. "Will you let him go or not?!"

"My dear wife, I have yet to understand how you convince me to do what I think is wrong. I do not understand why you believe letting our son go to a Christian home to celebrate the birth of a false messiah whose followers have caused us so much grief for the last two millennia, but when can I deny you? You so rarely ask for anything." Miriam barely curled her lips into a smile, but inside she was grinning. Her husband was a wonderful husband and father, but his ideas could be quite old fashioned.

She put her hands flat on the *sofah* and pushed on them to help her stand. She walked around the *sofah*. As she passed Moses, Miriam paused leaned over, and hissed her husband on the check. Then she stood erect, gave a gentle tug on her blouse to straighten it, and with measured steps walked to the room where her son lay curled on his bed weeping uncontrollably and her mother-in-law sat beside him stroking his back.

XVII

On January 6th, Alejandro's eyes popped open early in the morning. He lay still. Not a sound was heard. No, he realized he could hear his father snoring in the room next to his. It must be terribly early, he thought, so he turned over and went back to sleep.

A few hours later, Alejandro woke up because his father was shaking him awake. Alejandro looked at his father questioningly with one eye.

"It is time for *Shacharit*. Get dressed quickly," was all his father whispered and then he left the room. Alejandro was so excited about spending the day with Antonio that he was willing to wake early and go to the synagogue for morning *minyan*. He crept out of bed and got dressed as quickly as his shivering body would allow. Then he slipped out of the room as quietly as he could without waking his sisters. His father was at the door waiting for him, *tallit* bag in hand.

Moses could not help himself – he grinned. It had been over a year since he had walked to synagogue with his older two sons. He leaned over and ran his fingers through Alejandro's hair. The most pleasure in his son he would allow himself on this day, because he was so displease with Alejandro's day. Making the child get up early and go to *Sacharit* was his way of ensuring that the boy would not forget who he was. They left the house quietly, so as not waken the women.

After *Shacharit*, Moses and Alejandro returned home. Moses smiled as he walked in the house. He could hear his mother's *maniyas de tchaton* jingling as she stirred the coffee in the *ibrik*; it was a sound he heard since he was a baby. The whispers of the girls in their bed could be heard, as well. It was a typical morning in his house and he loved it. As they entered the kitchen, Miriam looked up from her place at the *sofah*. She was just tying her *yazma*. On her plate was some olives and pita; a chunk of feta with a knife on its plate was next to her plate. Moses and Alejandro walked to the sink and washed their hands. They walked in step to the *sofah* and sat next to each other. Miriam had to smile and wipe a tear from her eye. She had almost forgotten that David and Hiam had done the same thing when they had gone to *Shacharit* with their father. They had mimicked him, as well. Moses and his son said the *motzi* and then the four in the kitchen took a bite of pita. Hannah poured coffee for the adults and milk for the boy.

"Did you enjoy the *minyan* with your father?" asked Miriam.

"I guess," mumbled Alejandro, his mouth full of feta. Miriam looked at Moses and he raised an eyebrow and shrugged. Breakfast continued in the usual silence. When Moses and Miriam finished, they rose from their seats almost in unison.

As he was about to exit the room, Moses turned and said gruffly to his son, "Help your *Nána* until you go to Antonio's. You know the rules." And he was gone. Alejandro and his *Nána* turned to each other and grinned. They loved their time alone together, all the more because it was rare.

"Well, *inieto*, we need to start our chores," Hannah said with a grin on her face. She refused to name favorites among her grandchildren, but this one was.

"Absolutely *Nána*, where do we being?" her grandson asked as he stood up from the table and straightened like a soldier.

His grandmother got right into the game, "Private, first we must clear the *sofah* and wash the dishes and prepare for the next onslaught of the enemy."

"Yes, ma'am," Alejandro replied with a salute. He proceeded to stack the dirty dishes precariously on top of each other.

Hannah laughed, "*Inieto*, take the saucers out and put them on top of the stack. It works better."

"*Sí, Nána*," Alejandro responded as curtly as he could muster. Once he was ensconced at the sink with his sleeves rolled up and his grandmother's apron over his clothes, his sisters appeared for breakfast. They looked at him and each other and curled their lips inside their mouths to keep themselves from breaking out in laughter. They couldn't imagine a boy doing women's work, but they knew better than to comment about any goings on in their grandmother's kitchen. The image of their brother washing dishes was humorous enough, they couldn't talk the whole time they were eating. Instead, they were silent and when they were done they brushed their laps as they stood up, kissed their grandmother, and left for school.

Hannah could hear their giggles as they left the house. She brought the girls' dirty plates to Alejandro at the sink. She grabbed a dish towel and started drying the dishes. When they were done, Hannah started a new pot of coffee and had Alejandro put some cups on the counter.

"Now, *inieto* your *Bábu* said you were to study," Hannah reminded her grandson.

"Yes, ma'am" was his quick response. "I have. I have learned to wash dishes." His grin was enormous.

"So you have, Alejandro. And a quick study you are, but I believe your *Bábu* meant school work?"

"I should do my history. Can you help me, *Nána*?"

"My pet, I can listen, but I cannot read your book and I do not know all the history you do," Hannah answered sadly.

"Why *Nána*?" Alejandro asked innocently. "Do you need glasses?"

Hannah laughed, "Silly child. I do not think I need glasses. I can still sew a straight, perfect, hidden hem. I cannot read your book to you because I cannot read."

"What?" Alejandro asked. "Not read? Everyone can read."

Hannah grabbed Alejandro to her and gave him a passionate hug.

"I never went to school. When I was a girl we did not study like your sisters. We learned our prayers from our mothers and *Nánas*, along with everything else we needed to know." Alejandro stepped back from his grandmother and surveyed her with curious eyes. "I was always jealous of my brothers and boy cousins who went to school and learned about faraway places and how the stars move. Your *bábu* thought I would refuse the match with your mother because she was educated." Hannah laughed, throwing her head back in pleasure as she remembered this story. "I was thrilled! I could only hope she would teach me."

"But my *mame* did teach you to read, right?" Alejandro asked breathless.

"Oh, sweet *inieto*, even then I was too old and too busy to study. But your mother did teach me. She still does. Every week she reads me the newspaper. We discuss everything from international politics to science."

"But, my *Nána*, why not learn now?" Alejandro insisted.

Hannah grabbed her grandson again, "*Inieto*, I am even older now and I work just as hard. When you are as old as I am, you will see changing your ways is not easy. No, my time is gone, but you? You have the whole world ahead. You need to learn all you can," she stared at him hard as if to drill her belief into him. "Everything you can learn you must. You never know how you can be helped by what you learn."

Alejandro pondered his grandmother's wisdom. He believed everything she told him. She was a sage. He cocked his head and looked directly into the dark eyes, almost black, like olive pits, set in her wrinkled face. Then he leaned forward and kissed her wrinkled cheek. Without a word he went to his room.

Hannah heard him reading to himself. She smiled. Just then there was a knock at the door. Hannah rose from her chair and went to the door to let in her first customer of the day. Her neighbor Orpah was bringing fabric for her to make a dress. Hannah breathed deeply thinking how much she would relish this time to sit and gossip with her friends instead of working.

After Orpah left, Hannah checked on Alejandro. He had fallen asleep laying on his bed; his forehead was on top of the book he was reading. Hannah smiled and then gently sat on the edge of the bed.

Placing her hand on Alejandro's back, she shook ever so gently, "My littlest *inieto*, you must waken."

"uhm?" Alejandro drooled. "I was not sleeping *Nána*, really. I was studying."

"I believe you, my child. But you must get up and go to your friend's." Immediately, Alejandro jumped up and stepped into his shoes. "Slow down, my child. I must brush your hair and straighten your clothes." And she started doing just that. Alejandro sighed deeply, but knew better than to argue. "Now, Alejandro, should I walk you to your friend's house?"

Alejandro thought for a moment, "Please *Nána*, would you walk with me? I am not afraid I might get lost, but it is far and could be lonely."

Hannah got up from the side of the bed, "Well, I would love to. Come, we will need some scarves as well as our coats."

Once they were bundled to Hannah's satisfaction, they left the house hand-in-hand. The walk from the *Juderia* to the Italian neighborhood was not long. The grandmother and grandson strolled peacefully together.

When they arrived at an elegant house in the Italian neighborhood, they both paused at the front doors – two tall thin ones, similar to their own. Hannah and Alejandro looked at each other and marched up the two stairs to knock on the doors. A maid opened the doors and in Italian invited the pair in.

"Oh, no thank you. I will leave you with Antonio; I have to go home," Hannah replied in *Ladino* to the request she only understood because of the body language. She kissed Alejandro on the head and turned to go home.

Alejandro looked at the maid, swallowed his nervousness, and said in Italian, "My grandmother said she had to go home."

The maid smiled, "Come inside and I will take you to Antonio."

He walked through the doors and into an entirely different world. First the maid took his coast and scarf and laid them on a chair in the hall, then she showed him to the living room where everyone had gathered. Before she could announce the new guest, Antonio jumped up from his father's lap and ran across the room to greet his friend.

Alejandro didn't know where to look. The room was crowded with people dressed in the clothes his sisters admired in magazines. He didn't realize real people wore these clothes; Alejandro really thought they were only in pictures. He had never seen furniture so fancy, that matched. His parents' house was full of odd pieces of furniture that had been old even when his parents bought them. Antonio paraded his friend around the room introducing him to aunts and uncles, friends, government officials, and more people Alejandro would not remember. They finished the tour in front of Antonio's grandmother sitting on a settee like the matriarch she was. Alejandro realized that this woman looked nothing like his grandmother. She didn't seem tired or old, nor did she seem like the kind of person you could curl up in bed with and cry about the fight you had with your best friend or how mean your teacher was.

More amazing though was the object behind the matriarch. Alejandro could not be quiet as his friend led him to the grandmother.

"Antonio, Antonio, what is the ladder behind your grandmother?!" Alejandro demanded excitedly.

"Ladder?" Antonio was confused. "Oh the *ceppo*."

"Yea, it is pretty. What is it?" Alejandro asked trying to peer around the old lady on the settee who was looking at them both through her tortoise shell glasses with a disturbed look on her face. She couldn't figure out what they were saying because she was quite deaf.

"The *ceppo* is our symbol of Christmas," began Antonio. "Just like that funny candle holder is the symbol for your holiday. You know the one about war and the Temple in Jerusalem. Any way, the *ceppo* has three shelves to represent the three gifts. The bottom shelf always contains a *Presepio* to show the gift of G-d."

"Wait!" commanded Alejandro. "What is a *pre-presepio*? And which of G-d's gifts does it show?"

Antonio looked at his friend confusedly, "The *Presepio* is a depiction of the birth of Jesus in the manger. And what other gift could it represent than G-d's greatest gift – our savior?!"

Alejandro bit his tongue. He didn't think it was the time to explain that Jesus wasn't his savior.

Antonio continued, "Then there is a shelf with fruits and nuts to represent the gifts of the earth and finally a shelf with small presents to show the gifts of man."

"So," interrupted Alejandro, "what is the angel on top for? She is beautiful."

"Oh, she is!" agreed Antonio. "That was a gift to my grandmother from my grandfather. The angel represents hospitality."

A tall woman with her dark hair pulled up in a bun dressed in a red velvet dress came up behind the boys and stood between them. She put a hand on the shoulder of each boy.

"Antonio," she said gently, "have you given your friend the gift that *La Befana* left him last night?"

Antonio looked up at his mother, "Oh, *Mame*, I had forgotten. Come Alejandro..."

"Oh, no, my son," his mother interrupted him curtly. "First you must speak to your grandmother."

Antonio turned to his grandmother and spoke in a voice so loud Alejandro thought he was shouting to someone across the room, "Grandmama, this is my friend Alejandro!"

"Very nice to meet you," she said so quietly Alejandro didn't even think he had heard it.

Then Antonio grabbed Alejandro's hand and dragged him away. They went into the front hall and there on the chair next to the front hall table was a gift wrapped in blue fabric with a red ribbon tied in a large bow at the top around it.

"This is for you," announced Antonio.

"For me? What do you mean?" Alejandro inquired staring at this package hungrily. The only time he received presents unannounced was on his birthday and then they weren't so elegantly dressed. His family couldn't afford such luxury.

"Why?" Antonio repeated. "*La Befana* leaves presents for everyone on Epiphany."

Alejandro laughed, "Not everyone. Jews do not get gifts from *La Befana*. What is *La Befana*?"

Now it was Antonio's turn to laugh, "*La Befana*?! *La Befana* is a *who*, not a *what* and everyone knows who she is!"

"Just like everyone knows who the Maccabees are," reminded his friend smiling at having caught his friend out.

"Fine, fine," responded Antonio with a twinkle in his eye. "*La Befana* is a witch, but a nice witch. She is very old, even ancient, and bent and travels the world looking for the baby Jesus. You see, when Jesus was born she lived in the Holy Land and three kings went to visit the baby Jesus in Bethlehem. They kept asking for directions and asked *La Befana*. She told them she was too busy with her housework to help them. Later, she realized she should have shown them the way and visited Jesus herself. So she ran down the road after them. She never found them. She wanted to bring Jesus a present, so she visits every house that has children hoping to find Jesus. Since she is never sure if she has found him or not, she leaves a present for every child she sees."

Alejandro had been enchanted by the story.

"So this gift is really for me?" he asked breathlessly.

"Absolutely," smiled Antonio. "You must not insult *La Befana* by not opening her gift."

As Alejandro untied the ribbon, he asked, "So why do presents only arrive today? Why not everyday somewhere?"

"You do not know anything, do you? Today is Epiphany; the day the three kings gave their gifts to the baby Jesus."

Alejandro's response never made it to his lips. The cloth had fallen open and on the floor in front of where he knelt was a brand new book. Books were a rare and special gift. His birthday gifts were usually sweets or clothes, sometimes a new toy, but a book was for his *bar mitzvah* or school graduation. Carefully, he opened it and listened to the quiet crackle of the spine. Then reverently he lifted the book to his face and closed his eyes as he smelled it. All of his books for reading came from the library or his older siblings. All of them were old, ripped, and sticky. Antonio looked at his friend as though he were crazy.

"It is only a book," he commented.

"Only a book?" Alejandro nearly shouted. "A book is never 'only a book.' A book is a new place to wander. It is a new person to meet! I have never had a new book before. A book that is just mine and no one else's." Forgetting his friend, forgetting the elegant front hall he was in, Alejandro put the book on the floor in front of himself and began to read it. It was a storybook, an illustrated folktale from Italy. Antonio was so intrigued by his friend's absorption that he sat next to him and read as well. They lost track of time and never heard anything going on around them.

When Antonio's parents entered the hall from the party arm-in-arm, leading the guests, they stopped right in front of the boys.

Antonio's father cleared his throat and announced in a formal tone, though his eyes twinkled, "Young gentlemen, it is time to go the dining room."

"Yes, *Padre*, in a moment," was Antonio's automatic reply.

"No, son," reprimanded his father. "You are holding up our meal. The time is now." His wife put her hand gently on his arm to warn him about the tone of his voice.

The boys looked up and saw not only the imposing figure of the man of the house and his elegant wife, but all the guests are-in-arm behind them trying to be patient. Alejandro slammed the book shut and the boys stood up in unison, looking guilty.

"Come, my son," his mother commanded. The boys, holding hands, dashed over to Antonio's mother. Antonio took his mother's hand and the three Italians and one Jewish boy led the party into a dinner to celebrate the gifts given by the three kinds to the baby Jesus.

XVIII

That evening the family sat around the table with an oil lamp for light. The girls had their books out to do their homework, but instead they sat listing to Alejandro tell of his day.

"I promise *Bábu*, I was careful. I did not eat the sausage. Antonio's mother told me it was made with pork because pork represents good luck. I told her I had plenty of good luck, so I did not need the sausage." Moses laughed a deep belly laugh. *Nána* Hannah held her hand over her mouth as she laughed; she didn't like even her family to see her missing teeth. "Then there was a tray of stuffed noodles." Alejandro prattled on about, the stuffed noodles in rabbit sauce that smelled like heaven, but remembered his father's words and refused to eat it. "Because *Bábu* told me I could go, but I had to remember *Torah*."

"I hope you did not insult the hostess," worried his mother.

"Oh, *Mame*! *Nána* Hannah told me this morning to say I was full if I did not want to eat something. So that is what I said. That was not insulting, was it?" Alejandro suddenly felt very concerned. Antonio's mother had been only generous and kind to him.

"Alejandro, you continue to listen to your *nána*. She has years of wisdom in her head," responded his mother.

"Oh, good," he continued barely able to stop. "So then the maid brought a tray of grilled meat like chicken and pork. So I had a piece of chicken. "Finally, finally desert came! There were oranges and figs and *cenci*."

Hannah jumped in, "What is a *cenci*?"

"You know, *cenci* reminded me of *bumeulos*, except they were long strips and instead of syrup they had snow sugar on them.

"Powdered sugar, *inieto*," suggested his grandmother.

"Yes, powdered sugar. You see *cenci* means 'scraps of fabric' and that is what they look like. Like the bandages you make *Nána* Hannah when we get a cut. And the oranges are important as well. They represent sunshine." Moses opened his mouth to say something, but Alejandro never stopped. "And *La Befana* brought me a gift! A book! A brand-new-never-been-used book! Can you believe it? It is in Italian and it is all mine." And with that Alejandro was done. He had said all he could. Like a jug of water, he had poured himself empty.

The entire family sat for a few moments in silence. Alejandro had imparted an entire's day of excitement into the last fifteen minutes. Everyone was exhausted from the retelling.

Finally, Hannah spoke up, "Alejandro, may I look at your book?"

"No," commanded Moses. "I want to see it first."

No one had the courage to point out that he couldn't read Italian. Alejandro handed over this prized possession to his father. Even Moses wasn't going to admit he couldn't read Italian, so he slowly flipped through the pages looking at the pictures trying to discern any hint of overt Christianity. Everyone at the *sofah* watched him. No one spoke a word. Finally, he returned the book to his son.

"The illustrations are nicely done," was all he said. Then he got up from the *sofah* and left the room. Alejandro passed the book to his sister. Dora leaned over Hannah's shoulder and soon the two were absorbed in the book.

Miriam looked at her son, "Have you finished your school work?"

"No, *Mame*," was his answer and he too left the table to go to his room to find his school books.

"Girls. *Fijás*," she got no response, so with a knowing smile Miriam laid her hand across the open pages of the book. Now her daughters looked up. "I know you two still have homework." Suddenly, those two precious faces turned sad. "You may finish this book, but do not dawdle. Your homework must be done." And Miriam rose, as well, to leave. As she left the room, she turned back and said, "And do not forget your chores." However, she knew that last part wasn't heard because her daughters were already back absorbed in the story.

XIX

It didn't take long for the excitement of Christmas to wear off. The pressure of school kept the children occupied. Moses and Miriam found the job of trying to keep their grocery running more and more stressful. It wasn't that people didn't still need groceries, nor was it that they couldn't find suppliers; it was that people had less and less money to spend. That meant they had no money to give their suppliers or no money to bring home.

Moses' mother, Hannah, was not unaware of this. The money she had to run the household was less; every week, her son apologized for not giving her more. She had to stretch her *liras* much further. Meat was now reserved for *Shabbat*. Eggs were something she was learning to do without. Beans and rice and cheese and yogurt were what she could afford. The money David and Hiam sent could no longer be saved for treats or excursions; it was necessary for living everyday.

Hannah still did her sewing, but the women could not pay as much. Hannah accepted whatever payment her friends and neighbors offered, figuring some extra money was better than no extra money. Sometimes she even accepted barter, meaning her friends would bring something instead of money. There was her neighbor Leah who once brought two jars of homemade jam in exchange for having her older daughter's dress remade for the younger one. Her friend Rebecca brought enough fabric for two dresses, since her brother owned a fabric store, and only had one made. The rest Hannah could do with as she pleased. Hannah worried there wouldn't be enough money for new shoes for the children.

All three adults had agreed not to let any of the children know how difficult things were getting. Miriam and Moses continued their dialogues with their older sons through the mail as before. Filling the letters with family and town gossip, words of advice, and thank yous for the money they sent, but with the caveat that the boys shouldn't sacrifice for their family. Even though the children at home grumbled about the repetitious diet, it did not seem to occur to them that there was a reason for it. Moses, Miriam, and Hannah did without so the children would have clothes when theirs were too small and school supplies as they needed. These children were their future; the adults never said it, but all felt, that these three would probably end up leaving the island as well, someday.

Even though every family on the island, not just in the *Juderia*, felt the pinch, the *Juderia* was still filled with vibrancy. Visiting on *Shabbat* still happened, although the menus were somewhat curtailed. *B'nai mitzvah* were celebrated and wedding parties continued to fill the streets with music.

Tu B'Shvat arrived before Hannah expected it to, although it arrived the same time every year, the 15th of *Shvat*. Without many eggs or any sugar, she worried what sweets she could exchange with their family and friends. Luckily, the local honey was still available. Hannah searched her larder for bits of nuts and dried fruits and scrapings of jam at the bottom of jars. She bartered with friends and family for fresh fruit and eggs, in exchange for future sewing jobs. She even began questioning her youthful self for refusing a farmer as a husband because they would be so much better now if she had.

Finally, on *Tu B'Shvat* she had the kitchen table covered with plates of sweets. These plates each held *baklava*, *burmeulos*, slices of sponge cake, macaroons, *halvah*, *dulce de portokal*, and *dulce de lemon*.

The children begged for tastes, "Oh *Nána*, please just a teaspoonful of the *dulce*." Each whined and cajoled until Hannah lost all control.

"Out, get out of my kitchen!" she yelled, whipping her dish towel in the air. Dora, Hannah, and Alejandro fled the room with hurt looks on their faces.

"*Mio esfuegra*, what is the matter?" asked Miriam gently, trying not to upset Hannah any further. "I do not believe I have ever seen you so angry at the children." Hannah sat herself down heavily on a chair.

"Oh, Miriam," she began with a hint of despair in her voice. "I am at my end. I have scraped and saved and bartered and manipulated recipes to make these. And some I have hidden in the cupboards for *Purim* and *Pesaḥ*. After *Pesaḥ*, we will have no sweets left and I fear no money to buy honey – who even remembers sugar. This is all I can share with everyone. I hope they do not realize how little there is." And she put her face in her hands and wept.

Miriam looked around her. There were close to forty plates of sweets each beautifully laid out with an assortment of perfectly made and colorful sweets. Then she focued on one plate and realized her mother-in-law's distress. In year's past, those plates had been helped high and this year there was a single layer of food on each plate. She felt a pit in her stomach. Had their fortunes fallen so low?

"You have, as always, done an amazing job," Miriam enthusiastically said to her mother-in-law, hoping to hide her own fears.

Through her sobs, Hannah replied, "you forgot 'under the circumstances.'"

"Oh, no. No self pity in this house. That is what you told me when I married your son," reprimanded Miriam. "*Tu B'Shvat* is here and your sweets are some of the best in the *Juderia*. Do you think any one is so rich now that their plates are overflowing?" And Miriam put her arms around Hannah. This is how Moses found them when he entered the room; his mother with her head against Miriam's belly being comforted.

He walked up to them and asked, "Come, tell me who has died?"

By now Hannah had recovered her self-composure and pulled her face away from Miriam, wiped her eyes, and responded, "Our *Tu B'Shvat* treats are...are..."

"Delicious as always?" Moses tried half heartedly.

"So few," was his mother's weak response.

Moses smiled at his mother, "I would not worry that anyone will say anything. If they even notice. Everyone's pantry is a little stretched this year. We are being as generous as any family this year. *Mame*, it is time to send the children out. I have already seen a few others on the street." Hannah rose from her chair wiping her face, smiled weakly at her son, and walked to the sink to wash her face.

Miriam grabbed Moses' hand and squeezed it as she whispered, "We need to talk later." Louder, she said with much more confidence than she actually possessed at that moment, "I will get the *inyetos* ready to go out." And she left the kitchen. Moses walked up to his mother and hugged her from behind, as he had done many times when he was a child. This time, however, her head only came to his chest, rather than his head resting between her shoulder blades. He dropped his arms when he heard the children leaving their room.

"*Mame* says it is time to start taking the plates around," announced Alejandro.

"So it is," answered his grandmother.

"*Mame*, do I have to go this year?" asked Hannah hanging on her mother's arm. "I am too old." Her mother laughed a knowing laugh.

"If she is not going, neither will I," announced Dora.

"Enough!" commanded their father. "There is no way we are letting Alejandro go himself."

Hannah snapped back, "Are you worried he will get lost?"

"Oh not him," smiled her father, "the sweets. Do you really believe they will not find themselves in his stomach?" Everyone laughed.

"*Bábu* is right, *ermana*," said a smiling Hannah. "We cannot trust our own brother. I guess we will have to go." The sisters looked at each with grins. Their grandmother finished packing two baskets with plates, keeping some plates behind for visiting children, kissed each child, and handed them their *tallega*.

Hannah returned hers saying, "*Nána*, I am going simply to make sure the boy does not eat the treats. I am not hanging this bag around my neck to be filled with sweets. That certainly is for children!" And she stalked out of the kitchen. Dora and Alejandro hung their *tallegas* around their necks and scurried away after their sister.

"Children," announced Hannah to Moses and Miriam, "I am leaving you in charge. I need to rest." And with that, she left Miriam and Moses alone in the kitchen.

Almost immediately, there was a hesitant knock at the door. When Miriam opened it, she greeted a young cousin, took a plate off the table in exchange for one in the basket on the girl's arm, popped a treat in her *tallega*, and sent her on her way. For most of the afternoon, there were so many interruptions there was no time for husband and wife to talk.

XX

It was two days later, on *Shabbat*, before Miriam and Moses had a chance to talk. After *havdalah*, so it wasn't technically the Sabbath, they took an evening stroll to the beach. As they walked, side-by-side listening to the waves and feeling the cold fresh sea air, they spoke.

Hesitantly Moses began as if they were in the middle of a conversation, "It is not going well."

Miriam responded, "I did not know how hard this is on your mother."

Moses let out a sigh, "I am not sure what we can do. It is not possible to lower our prices, but people will not buy if we do not."

"They do not have any money to buy anything with," finished his wife.

"Without the business we have nothing."

"With the business we do not have much more."

"We could ask…"

"Oh, no!" jumped in Miriam. "Our sons have to live, too. If we ask them for more, then they will have that much less. Do we want Hiam to quit school?"

"But how can we feed ourselves?"

"There have been offers of marriage for Hannah. I have put my friends off saying she is too young, but I was around her age when we were betrothed."

Now Moses became stern, "And you say I cannot adjust to the modern world. She is too young; we promised our daughters they would finish school that is only two years for Hannah. We can make do for two years." He paused. "And what family in the *Juderia* can afford another mouth?"

Miriam turned her face away from her husband, "She would go abroad to their sons. Many families want to guarantee their daughter-in-law is *Rhodelisi*." Moses heard the pain in his wife's voice.

He grabbed his wife's arm, something he had never done before in a public place, and said with a terrible growl in his voice, "Never! No more separation. No more grandchildren without grandparents." Miriam knew not to argue nor did she want to She missed her brother far too much and still did not know anything about their baby. She turned to her husband with tears in her eyes as he dropped his hand from her arm.

"Tell me then," she pleaded, "how shall we feed our family?"

"I could go to the boys and get a job and send money to you, *Mame*, and the children," came his pained response.

She laughed, "And live in someone else's house? Who would make sure you eat enough fruit, or knows exactly how much sugar you like in your coffee?"

"I like sugar in my coffee? I had forgotten," he retorted with a crooked grin.

"This is not funny. I will not let you go. I cannot let the girls go, not yet. So how shall we feed our family?"

Now it was his turn to look away, out over the sea, and whisper, "I do not know."

XXI

The next month *La Fiesta de Purim* came with all the glorious festivities. Hannah made costumes for her three grandchildren. From a multitude of scraps she made her namesake a gypsy outfit. From an outfit Hiam left behind, she turned Dora into a boy, and her littlest grandson got his heart's desire to be a rabbi complete with beard and turban.

On the evening when Purim began, the children gleefully put on their costumes in their grandmother's room. Their grandmother sat in her chair, sewing kit in her lap, just in case there needed to be some final adjustments.

"*Nána*, you did it! It is so perfect," Hannah cried as she twirled her multi-colored dress in front of the mirror. Then she laughed, "No Dora, silly. You have the wrong hat. Come on, let us go see if *Bábu* has one you can borrow." Hand in hand, the girls turned to leave the room and stopped short and took a surprised breath.

There stood their parents dressed in the most elegant evening clothes the girls had ever seen. Their mother's forest green satin dress clung to her and went straight to the floor transforming their common mother into a movie star. She had styled her hair and placed an elegant hat on top. Her lips were deep bright red. As her daughters gasped and gawked, Miriam elegantly tucked a stray lock of hair on her neck back into her up do.

"Oh," cried both girls in union.

"*Mame*," sighed Hannah, "you look like a model in my magazines."

"No, like a movie star," murmured Dora.

"And what about your *Bábu*? Do I look like a *hamale*?" inquired their father throwing out his chest.

"*Bábu*, you look so handsome!" added Hannah quickly, surveying her father in a black suit with a white shirt, bowtie, and handkerchief crisply folded and tucked into his breast pocket.

Dora slipped in, "Not that you do not usually look handsome." And with that they all smiled.

Hannah had to know, "*Mame*, where did you get this gown?" Miriam turned to leave, looked coyly over her shoulder at her mother-in-law, and winked. She gathered the short train of her skirt in one hand and pulled her fur shawl tighter with the other.

"Come, all of you, we need to go hear the *Megillat Esther*," was all she would say. The girls followed her out trying to convince her to tell them the source of her dress.

Moses looked at his mother with a huge grin on his face, "*Mame*, you have done wonders again. I am constantly amazed at what you can do with your hands, what you can make out of nothing."

"*Bábu*, come on," nagged Alejandro. "We will be late!"

"Son, go help Dora pick out a good hat," was how Alejandro was shooed out of the room. "*Mame*, are you ready to go?"

"Do you remember, son, the things David wanted to be for *La Fiesta*? What an imagination. And Joseph's David. Always, always the same thing. He would ask me, 'Make me Mordechai'."

"Yes, *Mame*. I remember like it was yesterday. But this is today. Shall we go?"

She continued as if he had said nothing, "Your brother Jacob, had to be rabbi and then a soldier. And you. Always a farmer. Why a farmer? Do you remember why?"

"I had forgotten about that? I guess because there was something wonderful about living outside the *Juderia* and touching living things everyday. But come, *Mame*, it is time to go."

Hannah looked up at her son and smile, "Of course, we must go. I cannot miss this holiday where a woman saves the day through her quick thinking. Help me up! If we miss the start of the story, *mio inieto* will never forgive me." Moses did as his mother requested and offered her his hand.

The walk to the synagogue was not far, but it could have been for the multitude of characters on the streets. There were countless Queen Esthers, King Ahasueruses, and Mordechais. Some people even dressed like the evil vizier Haman. There were also those who had to be traditional and had swapped clothes – sisters looked like their brothers and a few brothers their sisters. And, of course, some people were a bit more creative. All over the *Juderia*, there was much laughter as friends enjoyed each other's costumes.

In the courtyard of the synagogue *Kahal Kadosh Shalom*, the family stood on the pebble mosaic medallion. Alejandro tried to negotiate himself to the very center of the sunburst design.

"Oh, little brother," said Dora in a disgusted manner, "it is too crowded for your silly nonsense. Come on!" And she tugged at his hand.

"No, I am going with *Bábu*," he responded. And so the family divided at the entrance to the synagogue. Moses and Alejandro made their way around the ground floor among the many kings, Mordechais, and evil Hamans to find *Nóno* Hiam. Despite his being at the synagogue frequently, Alejandro was still enamored with the traditional black and white pebble mosaic on the floor, the crystal chandeliers, and the gilt designs on the arches. It was a beautiful building.

Miriam, Hannah, and the girls made their way through the back room to the women's room. Here they stopped to admire their friends' and cousins' costumes. The room was small and crowded. *Nána* Hannah stopped to sit with her other daughter-in-law. Miriam chose to sit with her sister. Dora debated quickly if she wanted to squeeze herself nearer to the lattice covered window that separated the women's room from the main sanctuary so that she could hear the story better, or if she wanted to sit with her Aunt Alejandra. Her love for her aunt won the debate.

"Where's *Mame*?" she asked.

"You know she does not like coming to the *kahal* any more. She can barely hear us when we talk to her over the table, how can she hear anything in this noise and so far from the *tevah*?" responded her sister.

"True."

Now Alejandra turned to her sweet nieces, "Do you like my dress?"

"Your dress?" asked Hannah with her eyes wide. "Where did you get it?" Alejandra was about to say when she was hushed. The *hazan* had started reading the *megillah*.

Slowly the story of long ago Persia unfolded. The women were constantly hushing each other and the children as they strained to hear through the small opening. The opulent palace and the grand feasts appeared in front of the congregation like an oasis in the desert. The exile of Queen Vashti was accompanied by tasks of disgust at both for King Ahasuarus' improper request of his queen and his queen's refusal to do her husband's bidding. The girls always sighed when Esther was chosen as the new queen. What girl didn't want to be queen? Every time Haman's name was mentioned, the building exploded into a cacophony of foot stomping and pot banging. And it never failed that when the Jewish population of

Persia was saved by Esther convincing the king that they should live, the women's room erupted in applause.

Finally, the entire scroll was read and when it was finished, before it was even rerolled. The women started to stretch. Some with young children began to leave because their children were anxious to run around; they had sat for too long. Some chose to stay awhile because the spring night was cool and with all the women crowded into the tiny room, it was warm.

Almost immediately at the completion of the reading, Hannah resumed her conversation with her aunt, "*Tiya, mio tiya*, where did you ever find such an elegant dress?"

With her knees touching the chair in front of her, her sister on one side and her niece hanging over her, Alejandra realized there was no way she could escape.

Miriam looked at her sister, dressed in an odd assortment of Turkish robes and head gear in an attempt to look like the hero Mordechai, and smiled enjoying her sister's sense of discomfort, "Yes, *mio ermana*, where did you get this amazing decadent satin gown?"

Alejandra found herself studied by three anxious faces all with the same eyes and expressions.

"Oh, that old dress. It is something of a long story." And with that Alejandra leaned back in her chair, almost tilting it, and reached into a pocket hidden deep among the robes. She removed her compact and proceeded to powder her nose.

"*Tiya!*" demanded Dora at the end of patience. "THE DRESS!"

Her aunt replaced the compact and opened her mouth to speak, when from the other side of the window they heard a shout, "Alejandra, Miriam, come quickly! *Güestro padre!*"

The four rose as if they were one being and headed for the door, pushing chairs out of their way as they went. It wasn't easy with all the women and children milling around. However, these people did try to divide for them, just as the Red Sea had for Moses and Miriam. They zipped past *Nána* Hannah, oblivious of her presences. Dora dropped her father's hat in her haste, which *Nána* Hannah did manage to save from the crush of the crowd.

Alejandra happened to make it out of the women's room, through the passage and courtyard to the door of the main sanctuary before her sister.

She wasn't hampered by a long skirt, the freedom of trousers gave her speed. Once she fought her way through the doorway, she saw a clutch of men. They were huddled around an elderly man who was sitting on the floor. One, dressed all in black with a black turban, look around and saw her. He tapped the other men on their shoulders and they parted to reveal the elderly Hiam sitting on the floor his right hand on his temple holding up his head. Alejandra took two steps and dropped to her knees.

"*Bábu*," whispered Alejandra as she gently placed her hand on his shoulder.

He shrugged his shoulder to shake her off.

"Not in the *kahal*, *fija*," he said hoarsely.

"What happened?" demanded Miriam of her husband as she emerged from the crowd that had gathered at the door.

Her father looked up at her and said quietly, "I just slipped. I do not understand all this fuss." Alejandra attempted to help her father up. "Alejandra! I said, NO. You may not touch me in the *kahal*."

The sisters looked desperately at each other and then their husbands. Noah and Moses took places on either side of their father-in-law and lifted him up. They walked him home with their wives behind them and the girls behind them.

When Miriam and Moses came home later, they found Moses' mother waiting for them.

"What happened to your father, *ilmuera*?" she asked with much concern.

Miriam rested her hands on the back of a chair, "Nothing. He really did just slip. He is fine."

"I am very glad."

"He was not pleased with all the fuss. The look on Dora's face when Hiam came through the door being supported by his two sons-in-law was frightening," commented Moses.

"Yes, we decided *mio Mame* could deal with him. I believe I heard her say something to him about drinking too much, even for *Purim*," added Miriam.

Hannah smiled, "I know how much he likes being fussed over. I put the children to bed. We should go, too. Tomorrow the fair begins and you know the children will be up early."

XXII

The next morning Hannah, Dora, and Alejandro met their grandmother in the kitchen; they were so anxious to get to the fair.

"Hurry, *Nána*, hurry! We have to get there early," urged Dora as her grandmother was shuffling around the kitchen in her *patuklas*.

"What is the hurry? The venders have yet to set up their stalls," responded her grandmother. "Besides, you must wait for your parents."

At that moment, Moses came bursting into the kitchen.

"*Mame*, hurry, the fair will start without us!" exclaimed their father. The children stared at him in shock. He was usually a calm, even, unhurried person.

His mother looked at him and in a mocking reprimand said, as she shook hand making her *maniyas de tchaton* rattle, "*Fijo*, what is the hurry? Sit, eat your breakfast."

"But *Mame*," whined her son. And then the two started laughing. They laughed so hard that Moses had to help his mother to a chair. The children continued to stare. They could not imagine what was so funny.

"Now, my children, do not bother your grandmother any more. Do you understand how much you nag her," commented Moses, not ungentely, once he could breathe again.

At that moment, Miriam walked in.

"What is so funny," she asked as she took her seat dressed as her usual self without satins, furs, or make-up.

"Nothing, *Mame*," mumbled Dora through a mouthful of feta.

"Now children, we can all enjoy the fair on *La Kay Ancha*. Please this year, let us stay together. I do not want to spend my evening trying to find the three of you in different parts of the *Juderia*, again. Last year's fair lost some of the fun with that act."

"Oh, *Mame*," moaned Hannah. "I am too old to follow you around like a *niña*. Sarah and I and some of the other girls were going to take a buggy to *Puerta de la Mar*. Now the fair will be no fun." And with that she put down her fork, and sat back in her chair with a pout on her face.

"Hannah, go have fun with your friends. You are right; you are getting old enough, but stay with Sarah." Hannah sat up straight and began eating again. And then Miriam turned to Alejandro, "but you, little man, will stay with your *padre* and me." Alejandro made a face, but knew better than to protest.

"What about me?" asked Dora.

Miriam and Moses looked at each other for a few moments. Miriam bit her lower lip on one side. Moses raised one eyebrow.

Moses drew in a breath, "You, little *fija*, will go nowhere without asking."

"*Bábu,*" began Dora.

"You heard your *Bábu*, Before you run off with your friends, we need to know. And you need to check in with us. Yes?" commanded her mother.

"Yes, *Mame*," replied Dora not as pleased with the outcome as she would have liked, but knowing that she would convince them no further.

Moses turned to his mother, "*Nána*, are you coming with us?"

"I do not know," she said. Then with a wicked grin *Nána* Hannah asked, "Do I have to stay with you or can I go off with my friends?" Miriam started to giggle, as did the children.

Moses cleared his throat as he thumped his chest with his fist as if he was trying to clear it, "Well…*Mame*, I think we can trust you to find your way home."

"But you have to check in," added Dora. Everyone laughed.

Once they had finished breakfast, the girls cleaned the *sofah* and washed the dishes, so that their grandmother could finish dressing. Miriam swept the kitchen floor and sent Alejandro to make his bed. When the morning chores were finished and *Nána* Hannah was ready, they left for the fair on *La Kay Ancha*. Each of the children took some coins with them that they had saved up.

"I wonder if we will see *Tiya* Alejandra and *Tiyo* Noah," pondered Dora.

"We always do. Why?" asked her sister with much curiosity.

"Because they always have some spare change for us to buy treats with," she commented with a grin.

"Oh, I thought it was because they are fun and you love them," replied Hannah haughtily. Then she smiled at her little sister, "but the treats are good, also."

The discussion of the treats made Alejandro crave some.

"*Bábu*, can we get snow cones?" he asked. "Please?"

And before their father could answer, Dora started, "Can I get some *bourekas*?"

Miriam and her mother-in-law looked at each other in horror, each wondering where the money would come for these treats. Then from around the corner came *Nóna* Hiam and *Nána* Dora.

"*Padre*! *Mame*! I am so glad you are coming to the fair," exclaimed Miriam upon seeing her parents.

"*Fija*, I have never missed the *La Fiesta* fair since I was born," commented her mother. "Why should I now?" And then she added, "*Purim, Purim, lanu pesach en la manu.*" (Purim, Purim is already ours, Passover almost at hand.)

Hannah turned to Hiam, "Are you fine now? We were worried about you last night."

Before he could say a word, his wife remarked wryly, "He fell because he was drunk, but he will not admit to that. I keep telling him, just because the rabbis say he should drink does not mean he should drink as much as his sons-in-law." Miriam and Moses winked at each other and bit their lips.

"*Nóno*, are you really going to be fine?" asked Alejandro with much concern. He had had problems going to sleep because he was so worried about his favorite grandfather. Although as he was trying to be a big boy, he wouldn't admit that to anyone.

Hiam looked down at his grandson and then took his hand, "Yes *inieto*, I am fine. I bumped my head, but everyone does when they fall."

Alejandro squeezed his grandfather's hand, "I am so glad!"

"I am too," agreed his grandfather. "You know, *mio inieto*, I need your help at that table of fortune. Will you come and help me? You will bring me good luck." And Hiam started to walk away with the boy.

"Wait, *Nóna*," commanded his grandson. "*Bábu*, may I go with *Nóna*?"

Moses had to smile.

"Yes, *fijo*, you may go with your *nóna*." Al they turned to go, he added, "Have fun! Bring him back when you are through, and not too late please, *esfuegro*."

Miriam added under her breath, "And do not let your *nóna* get lost." Only her husband heard her and he snorted, then covered his smile with his hand.

The elder Dora and Hannah fell in pace behind the younger set and gossiped. Miriam slowed her pace so they could keep up.

"Sarah! Sara! Wait for me!" called out Hannah who say her best friend at th enxt corner. "*Mame*, there is Sarah. I will find you later." And she was off running to catch up with her friend.

The "have fun" her mother called out after her was never heard.

Moses looked at his wife, "You know it has been a long time since you and I have taken a buggy ride on *La Fiesta*. How about I take my beautiful *espoza* on a ride to *Guerta de los Limones*?"

Miriam turned to her mother and mother-in-law, "*Proves I gaviyentos.*" (He's poor, but acts like he's rich.)

Moses looked at his wife slyly, "*Lo ke no se fada en la boda, no se ase toda l'ora.* (If you do not take advantage when available, you may miss out.) It is not often I have the chance to treat you, let me worry about the riches needed to treat my wife, whose value is far above that of rubies. Will you go with me?"

Miriam looked at her husband coyly, "I do not know. I believe you must ask my mother."

Dora looked back and forth at her parents. Obviously, they were having some secret conversation. Suddenly, she realized she may be left with her grandmothers, whom she loved, but that was no way to spend a day at the fair.

"What about me?" she interjected?

"I do not know," answered her father. "Do you think your mother would allow you to take a buggy ride with an older gentleman?"

Now Dora got into the game, "I do not know. You should probably ask her mother."

Moses grinned. It wasn't often he was relieved of the pressures of the world and could spend a day having fun. He stopped and turned to face the older women.

"Excuse me, *esfuegra*. May I interrupt?" Moses started very politely. "I would very much like to take your lovely *fija* and *inieta* on a buggy ride. May I have your permission?"

The two women stopped their stroll and chatter.

"Hannah, what do you think?" asked Dora.

"Eh, she is a grown woman and can watch her own daughter. I would let them go, so we can have some peace for a change," responded her companion. And then they both cackled at their own foolery.

Moses' eyes started to gleam, "*Rengrasyo te.*" He turned on his heel, took his daughter's hand, nodded at his wife, and headed towards the fair with his two dates. There he found a line of buggies and their horses festooned with flowers.

The drivers were calling out, "*Ir i venir un grosh.*" (To go and return for one grosh.)

Moses stopped one of the drivers and motioned Miriam and Dora in as he asked the driver to take them to *Guerta de los Limones*.

As they enjoyed the ride to the Turkish quarter, Dora couldn't contain her curiosity, "*Bábu*, why is the *Guerta de los Limones* only opened on the Jewish holidays."

"No, *fija*, that is not true. It is open every day, but only open to the Jews on the Jewish holidays."

"That does not seem right."

"No, it does not."

Back at the fair, Hannah and Sara bought *bourekas* and *shish kebabs* with their pooled funds. Then they met up with some more friends at the line for the buggies. Five girls piled into the buggy and headed toward *Puerta de la Mar.*

"What is in your basket?" inquired Rebecca, a short plump girl with curls.

Sarah pulled back the napkin covering the contents to reveal the warm food inside.

"Wow!" shouted Regina, a blond giggly girl.

"Let me see! Let me see!" squealed Rebecca. "Oooooo, yummy. Is that for all of us?"

"Of course. I thought we were all bringing something, what did you bring," inquired Hannah.

Sunny laughed. Her name really wasn't Sunny, but since she was Sarah's cousin and had the same name, Hannah had named her for her cheery smile and hair that turned gold in the summer sun.

"No one asked what was in my bag," chirped Sunny. When she opened it the other girls "oohed" and "ahhed" over the three bottles of lemonade.

"Yea! I love my *tiya's* lemonade," applauded Sarah. "What did you bring, Rebecca?"

"*Desayano de deso*," was her happy response.

"And you, Regina?" queried Hannah.

Her response was a single word, "*fullar.*"

All the girls sucked in their breath in a chorus of "ahh."

"I believe we have a perfect feast," announced Dora.

Finally, they reached the gate and made the driver promise to collect them around noon. Then they took their baskets and an old blanket that Sunny had brought and made their way down to the beach.

"Where are we going to settle?" asked Sunny.

"Over there, by the dune," suggested Regina. Having decided that, Sunny and her cousin tossed out the blanket and the girls settled down to chat and nibble until they had to go home.

XXIII

Just before noon, they gathered their baskets, napkins, and blankets and headed back to the gate where their buggy was waiting. The five girls clambered in to go home. When they reached *La Kay Ancha*, the girls thanked the driver and climbed down. After hugs all around, the girls divided up to go home.

"See you all later! *Hag Purim*," called Hannah as she turned towards home. As she spun around, she saw her grandmother's also headed towards her home. "*Nána* Hannah, *Nána* Dora, wait for me." She ran to catch-up.

"*Inieta*, did you have a nice morning by the sea with your friends?" inquired *Nána* Hannah.

"It was lovely," responded Hannah with a broad smile across her sun-reddened face.

"Who did you go with?" asked *Nána* Dora as Hannah took her place between her two grandmothers.

"Oh Sarah and her cousin Sarah and Rebecca and Regina."

"Oh how nice! I remember going to the beach with my friends for *La Fiesta*. We would site on a blanket and enjoy the first nice days on the beach, talk about life, and laugh," reminisced her namesake. "Did you do that too Dora?"

"Oh yes," sighed Dora. "Tell us, what did you, girls, talk about."

"Sarah was telling us about her *despaozado* and how he is saving money to send for her. It sounds so romantic."

Nána Dora broke in, "I am sure it does, but to be a new bride is not easy. I wonder how she thinks she will do it far from her mother and grandmothers."

"To be a wife at any stage is not easy," piped in *Nána* Hannah.

"You just do not understand," was Hannah's exasperated response. "You are too old to remember love and romance."

"*Mia inieta*," *Nána* Hannah said, "you are never too old to remember love and romance. It has simply been colored by practicality and pain."

Nána Dora patted the girl's arm, "Tell us about Sarah's plans." And Hannah did all the way home until they arrived at the house unaware of the movement of their feet.

The three were the first back at the house. There they set the *sofah* for *Seuda de Purim*. The elder Hannah began to prepare the beef she had left earlier in the day marinating in olive oil, lemon juice, salt, pepper, and marjoram.

Contemplating the best way to stretch what she had, she called over Dora, "Help me cut this meat to put on the skewers."

"*Shish kebabs?*" queried Dora.

"It seems like the best idea," answered the other. Then she began cutting onions into wide wedges. The two women worked as a team skewering onions and meat. It took them almost no time to have the job done. In the mean time, their granddaughter had set the charcoal brazier up in the courtyard.

"Should I start the coals?" she asked.

"Oh no my dear, let one of us do that," responded *Nána* Hannah as she headed toward the courtyard. Once by the brazier, she gathered the coals in a pile and put a match to them. First the flame was high, but it slowly died and the coals began to warm.

"Hannah, watch the coals. Make sure they slowly turn white. If you have any problems, just call me." Then she left the courtyard and returned to the kitchen.

There she took some pita from yesterday and piled them on a plate.

"Hannah, where are your lemons?" asked Dora.

"Come, Dora, sit at the *sofah*. The lemons are there and it will be easier to cut them," said Hannah as she directed the other elderly lady. And that is how Moses, Miriam, and Dora found them when they arrived home – sitting at the *sofah* cutting lemons into wedges.

The three came in laughing hysterically.

"*Fijo* what is so funny?" asked Hannah.

"Yes, *yerno*, tell us so we may laugh as well," chimed in his mother-in-law.

Moses drew a breath to calm himself and couldn't.

So Miriam began the story, "We came back from the garden..."

"It was so lovely and smelled so fresh," piped in Dora.

"And decided to wander the fair," contained Miriam as if she'd never been interrupted. "While we were wandering about, we bumped in *Rabbi* Reuben Eliyahu Israel."

Nána Dora gasped, "The chief *rabbi*!"

"And he...and he...," Dora was still laughing so hard she couldn't finish her sentence.

Moses continued the story, now that he had regained control of himself, "And he insisted that Dora was a boy. He kept asking who she was because he could not quite recognize her."

Dora flung her arms around *Nána* Hannah, "Thank you for my costume! It is perfect!"

"It was not until Dora took off her cap that he finally believed she is a girl," concluded Miriam. Having completed the story, the three sat down at the *sofah*. Dora flung her cap, which she had been carrying, on the table and shook her head letting her black wavy bobbed hair fly free.

Unbeknownst to them, *Nóno* Hiam and Alejandro had come in behind them. Having heard the story, Hiam's face was dark.

"I do not like the idea that you dressed as a boy, Dora. Fooling the chief *rabbi* is not proper," he growled.

Always with a question, Alejandro asked, "What makes the chief *rabbi* the chief *rabbi*?"

Moses beckoned his son over to him. When Alejandro was standing in front of his father, Moses put his hands on the boy's shoulders and began:

"*Rabbi* Rueben Eliyahu Israel is a wise and learned man. He comes from a long line of rabbis; in fact, 200 years worth of rabbis, but that makes him neither wise nor learned. Before he became chief *rabbi* for the *Juderia*, he was the *rabbi* of the *Sephardim* of Romania. Romania is a country in Europe. While he was there, he translated some prayers and famous Jewish books into *maestro espanoil* because he wants to make sure that even those who do not know Hebrew, understand their prayers. Even King Victor Emmanuel knows our chief *rabbi* to be a great man – he knighted *Rabbi* Israel."

"So he is Sir *Rabbi?*" interrupted Alejandro. That made everyone giggle.

"Yes, I guess it does. The Italians helped Rabbi Israel found the *Collegio Rabbinico Couvitto.* He is a chief *rabbi* because he is a leader and is preparing us to be part of the world."

All Alejandro could say at the end of this monologue was, "oh." And then he returned to things important to his world, "*Nóno* and I had a great morning! We won the games. Not all the games, but a lot of them!"

"I said he would be my good luck charm," Hiam added as he sat down.

"And how many sweets did you eat?" asked his wife.

"Not too many," Alejandro chimed in. Miriam laughed, but gave her father a dirty look.

"How much money did you win?" asked Moses.

"More than I spent." And he threw a handful of coins on the table.

"*Nóno,* wow!" exclaimed the boy as he reached across the table to get them.

"No, me!" squealed Dora.

Hiam slammed his hand on the table. The children pulled their hands back.

Hiam looked at his grandson, "I said that I would divide the winnings among the three of you after dinner. Now run along."

The two children looked at each other, at the other adults at the table, and decided that it was time to leave the room. As they walked toward their, the adults around the table could hear them discussing their morning's activities.

"Hello? Hello?" was heard in the hall.

"Come to the kitchen," called out Miriam too tired to move. In came Noah and Alejandra with a basket of food. As they started unloading bottles of wine and bowl of tomato and cucumber salad, Hannah came into the kitchen.

"*Nána* Hannah, I think the coals are done," she announced. Then Hannah noticed her aunt and uncle, "*Tiya, Tiyo* you made it! *Tiya,* I have so much to tell you."

"Well then, I believe we should take the kebabs and go in the courtyard and cook them and talk," commented her aunt as she handed her husband the basket and grabbed the plate of meat for herself and the plate of pita for her niece. Arm-in-arm, the two went to the courtyard. Barely out of the door, they were already deep in conversation.

Nearly half an hour later, the aunt and niece returned with warm slightly charred pita and hot, fresh grilled kebabs. The other adults had been sitting around the table chatting and drinking.

Alejandra looked at those around the *sofah* and the empty bottle of wine before she spoke.

"Did you save any wine for me?" she laughed.

"Is it all cooked?" Dora asked her daughter.

"Yes, it is. Should I go get Dora and Alejandro?"

"Oh no, *ermana*, you sit since you have done the cooking," said Miriam. "I will go get the children." Then she rose, a bit unsteadily, and left the kitchen.

As she moved toward the door, her sister finished setting the *sofah*. When Miriam returned a complete *Seuda de Purim* was awaiting her.

"They had fallen asleep on the same bed. I guess their morning was more exhausting than we thought," Miriam said. "But once I said *Tiyo* Noah and *Tiya* Alejandro were here, they said they would get up. They should be here in a moment." Barely had the words come out of her mouth, then the children came barreling out from behind her.

"*Tiya*! *Tiyo*!" they squealed as their aunt and uncle made room for them at the table.

And so the extended family sat down for the afternoon to eat and share stories and celebrate the cunning of Queen Esther, before they returned to their every day lives the day after next.

XXIV

Three weeks before *Pesah* began only a week after *Purim*, the elder Hannah and Dora, and Miriam and Alejandra sat in the courtyard of Miriam and Moses' house sipping their coffee and cracking pistachio nuts in their teeth. This wasn't just a social call for Alejandra and Dora, not that they really needed an excuse to visit. They stopped in regularly to gossip with Hannah and Miriam, play cards with the girls, and dote on the boy. This was a family meeting. Alejandra and Noah's business was still going fine, but Miriam and Moses' was failing badly.

"We certainly do not live lavishly; people just are not spending money like they did last year. And I know I said that last year, but this year is worse. However, we certainly are not hungry," Alejandra told them.

"I do not understand why our grocery is doing so badly," sighed Miriam. "We have reached the point where it is barely worth opening in the morning."

"The two of you may have time to debate the wonders of business, but I have more urgent matters," interjected Hannah. "*Pesah* is coming. I need to feed six people for eight days, not to mention two *seders*. Do we know how many will be here for that? How am I to do this? On top of that my *inieto* needs new shoes for school and Dora needs a new school skirt. Really, she is too old to be seen in a skirt that short."

"I know, *esfuegra*, please," pleaded Miriam. As much as she shared with her sister and mother, she had never explained how difficult things had become in their home.

"Shoes? A skirt? Come now, *ermana*, why do you not tell me these things? Those Noah and I can do for you," jumped in Alejandra. Dora remained silent, she never dealt with money, and her husband had always handled their business even for the house. Besides, she was rather deaf and couldn't follow the conversation very well.

Miriam breathed deeply, "We cannot ask you to raise our children."

"They are our children, as well!" Alejandra spat at her sister. "After ten years of trying do you think we will every have our own? Give me a touch of your pleasure." And she grabbed her sister's hand. Miriam squeezed that proffered hand as if it was pulling her from the sea.

"But what of *Pesaḥ*?" asked Hannah.

Alejandra turned to her sister's mother-in-law, "We should consider this a larger family, maybe one of eight or ten. What do we *all* need?" The three family leaders knew that this meant Alejandra and Noah would do the bulk of the purchasing, but they had to have food for *Pesaḥ*. So they planned.

"Now that we have solved that," commented their mother when the planning was done, pleased to see her daughters still so bound, though she had no idea what the disagreement had been about, "can we have some more coffee?"

The next morning began *Pesaḥ* preparations in earnest. Once the children were off to school, Hannah and Miriam took out their cleaning supplies. Since business was slow at the store, there was no need for Miriam to go there. Besides, all the other women would be spending their days until *Pesaḥ* began preparing for the holiday. This was why Hannah could devote her time to the preparation – the majority of her customers would be too busy to bring their mending to her.

The women began with beds. Each bed was stripped, the mattress was inspected, repaired, aired for the afternoon, and turned when it was put back. Then the winter quilt was inspected for necessary repairs and then hung out in the courtyard for airing before being packed away until next winter. The list of chores to be done was endless, white washing the house inside and out, scrubbing the *seshicos*, changing the dishes, and boiling the glasses and knives to make them *kosher* for *Pesaḥ*.

Each day Hannah and Dora would come home and one of them would declare, "*De Purim a Pe Pesah sah...major ke mi madre no me pariera!*" (From *Purim* to *Pesaḥ*, I wish I had never been born!)

They barely had time to drop their books on their bed before their grandmother or mother called to them, "Change from your school clothes into some old ones. I need your help."

Some days, the girls would go to school with homework unfinished, but they certainly weren't the only ones. In fact, some of their friends missed a number of days of school because of the preparations for *Pesaḥ*. There came one day when even Hannah and Dora missed a day of school.

At the beginning of the week, *Nána* Hannah had rolled up the *tapeties*. Now that the floors had been scrubbed, walls white washed, and furniture polished, it was time to wash the rugs before they were put back down. So early one Thursday morning less than a week before Pesaḥ, a buggy arrived at the front door. While Miriam loaded the *tapeties* into the buggy, *Nána* Hannah finished loading a basket with a picnic. Alejandro watched her while munching on his breakfast. Dora entered the kitchen as she finished buttoning her blouse.

"*Nána*, have you saved me some breakfast?" she asked.

"*Inieta*, find something and come quickly, the buggy is here," her grandmother answered distractedly. Dora grabbed a hunk of feta in one hand and some olives in the other and wandered outside. "*Inieto*," commanded his grandmother, "help me carry these two baskets out to the buggy."

Alejandro stuffed his last bite of pita into mouth and dutifully grabbed a basket and followed his grandmother to the buggy. There was his aunt, other grandmother, and sister Hannah loaded with the *tapeties* from Alejandra and Dora's home trying to squeeze them into the buggy while leaving room for all them to climb in as well. When all the *tapeties* had been stuffed into the buggy, the four women and three children climbed in. Once in, they balanced baskets of food and stiff brushes.

The buggy took them to the sea. There everyone piled out and Miriam and Alejandra quickly unloaded the *tapeties*. Everyone took a bundle or a basket and they trouped to the sea.

"Finally," said a still sleepy Dora, "we are here. Now I can lay on the rocks and nap."

Hannah giggled. Their mother did not find humor in this at all.

"*Inieta*, this is not a time to be lazy," she said sternly. "We need to scrub these *tapeties*. If I thought you were not going to help, I would have sent you to school."

"But *Mame* this is so tedious! Who like to scrub rugs?" whined the younger daughter.

Her mother reprimanded her with, "A young lady who is a good daughter and helps her mother prepare for *Pesaḥ*."

Hannah and Dora looked at each other and rolled their eyes as they untied the string holding the rugs closed. Then they took a rug and brush down to the edge of the sea and scrubbed it.

"Dora! Hold on tighter," commanded Hannah.

"I am holding on as tight as I can," Dora yelled back. "You try keeping your hands on this as the waves pull it out."

"Girls! Girls!" interrupted their mother. "Work it out peaceably, but work it out. We have to get through all of these this morning." And she turned back to the rug she was scrubbing, one bare knee holding it still as she scrubbed.

As each *tapesty* was completed, it was laid on the rocks to dry.

"Amazing," commented Alejandra to Alejandro, who had been helping her, "how quickly this all gets done when we work together."

"This was fun," he responded looking down on his soaking feet and trousers. His aunt had tried numerous times to roll them up, but they fell each time and she had given up.

His aunt smiled, "it was fun because we did it together."

Miriam looked up as she put her last rug down, "Are we finished?"

Her mother stood up slowly rubbing her hands on her lower back, "I believe so."

The senior Hannah wiped her forehead with the back of her wrinkled hand, "Thank heavens! I just do not know if I could scrub one more."

The three women looked at each other and sighed; then in unison, without intention, they hollered, "Children! Children!" Laughter erupted among them.

From the edge of the waves, the three children and their aunt came running.

"About time!" exclaimed Alejandra. "We were beginning to believe we would dine without you." Then she threw herself down on the sand.

Hannah and Dora started grabbing baskets from the shady spot behind the rocks.

"Alejandro, help with the blanket," commanded Hannah.

The two laid out the blanket and then Dora put baskets around to hold the blanket down. Thankfully, the two elderly women sank down.

"Hannah," Dora said to her compatriot, "I have no idea if I will ever be able to get up from here."

Hannah smiled weakly and responded, "If I get up, I will try to help you."

"*Nána* Dora," asked Dora, "are you hungry? Should I pour you some lemonade?"

And so the feast began. When they finished the food, Miriam reached up to the rug over head and felt it.

"Well, the *tapeties* are not yet dry," she said dejectedly.

"Awe," the children chimed in.

"What shall we do?" asked *Nána* Hannah with mock distress.

Nána Dora smiled slyly and took a deck of cards out of the bottom of one of her baskets. Her partner raised an eyebrow and grinned.

In response to her grandmother, Dora grabbed an empty lemonade bottle and ran down to the waves. She filled the bottle, dashed back up the sand, placed her fingers over the top, and shook a shower of water over her little brother. He jumped up and immediately began to chase her across the beach.

"Come on, Hannah," he called over his shoulder. "Help me!" Alejandra and Miriam looked at Hannah.

"Oh, really," snorted Hannah, "That is so childish." She chose instead to stay with her mother and aunt and chat.

When the *tapeties* had finally dried, the five women shook them out and carefully rolled them up on the picnic blanket to keep as much sand as possible off of them. Then they called the children. Everyone took some *tapeties* and baskets and headed towards the street to meet the buggy to take them back to the *Juderia*.

XXV

On March 31st in the evening, Moses went into the house and returned to the courtyard with a candle in a candlestick.

He said with much formality, "It is time for the *Kalhamira*." Then he lit the candle. "Come Alejandro, I could use some help," he continued and handed his son an empty dish.

Before they entered the house, Moses recited the blessing for the removal of the *hamets*, "*Baruch atah adonoy elohanu melech ha-ohlam, ahsher kid-shahnu b'meetzvohtahv ahl-bee'oor hamets.*" (Blessed are you, Lord our G-d, Ruler of the universe, who has sanctified us with Your commandments and commanded us to remove *hamets* from our possession.)

Then in complete silence, room by room, Moses and Alejandro searched for any scrap of bread, any hint of cake, any piece of food that might contain any leavening agent. Under every piece of furniture, behind every curtain, and under each *tapety* Moses hunted. Every crumb he found, he put in the dish. When every corner had been checked, they returned to the courtyard. Alejandro handed his mother the dish filled with bits of *hamets* and Moses stated, "*Cahl hameerah d'eehah veer'shootee, d'lah hazeeray ood'lah vee'ahr'ray vahteel v'hahsheev k'ahp'rah d'ahr'ah.*" (May all *hamets* in my possession which I have not seen or removed be annulled and considered as the dust of the earth.)

"*Rengrasyote*," she said as she rose to receive the dish.

"Good, now we can finally eat inside again," Dora commented to break the solemnity of the moment. Her grandmother gave her a disgusted look.

Miriam turned to her family and suggested, "Tomorrow is a very long day. I think we should all go to bed early. I am." She then turned and went into the house, carrying the dish with her. The family sat in silence and then followed her in.

In the morning, Miriam got dressed in some older clothes and took the dish to the courtyard and carefully burned every piece of *hamets* in it. When it was ash she recited, "*Cahl hameerah d'eehah veer'shootee, d'lah hazeeray ood'lah vee'ahr'ray vahteel v'hahsheev k'ahp'rah d'ahr'ah.*" (May all *ḥamets* in my possession which I have not seen or removed be annulled and considered as the dust of the earth.) Then she went to the kitchen to eat breakfast with her mother-in-law. One by one, the children joined them. Moses had left of the store already.

Before the family had finished their breakfast, Alejandra and her mother arrived with baskets of food.

"Children, finish breakfast quickly," commended their grandmother. "Hannah, wash the dishes. We have a lot to do and only today." And that was basically the end of breakfast.

Hannah whisked the dishes to the sink to be washed, literally taking a glass out of her brother's hand.

"Hey! I was drinking that," Alejandro protested.

"To bad," she responded over her shoulder. "I have to wash these dishes. No time to wait."

While this was going on, their grandmother had started to unpack the baskets. Miriam stood in the center of the kitchen surveying the scene before starting on a course of action.

"*Mame*, let us put the wine over there in the corner. That will leave more room for us to work," she started to direct. "Before we unpack anything else we must finish the kitchen."

Hannah heaved a big sigh over the dishes in the sink. *Nána* Hannah came from her room lugging an old sheet.

"Alejandra, be so kind as to help me put a tablecloth on the *sofah*," she panted.

Alejandro asked, "*Mame*, what is the fuss about the kitchen?"

Dora laughed, "You ask that every year!"

"Shhh," hissed her mother as her *yazma* slipped down her face.

"*Inieto*, the dishes must be changed every *Pesaḥ* and then again when *Pesaḥ* is over. Special food requires special dishes," commented his *Nána* Hannah gently. "Now, go to the store and tell your *padre* that your *mame* won't be in today. See if he needs any help."

"Yes, *Nána* ," he said as he was almost out the door.

"*Mia esfuegra*, I believe my husband knows I am staying home today to finish the *Pesaḥ* preparations," Miriam said accusingly.

"Oh, *mia ilmuera*, we all know that...except maybe Alejandro," laughed Hannah. "I do not want him in the kitchen as we swap dishes around. Do you?"

Miriam sat on a chair, "No, you are right."

"*Ninas*," commanded their grandmother. "Why are you just standing there? Dora get the ladder and start taking all the dishes out. Hannah, now that you have finished the dishes you can accept the dishes from your sister. And Alejandra, take the dishes and stack them here on the *sofah*."

"And *Nána* Hannah," inquired Dora, "what are you going to do?"

"Me?" responded Hannah rather indignantly. "I am going to sit here with my friend Dora and watch. We are old women you know."

At that comment both Miriam and Alejandra covered their mouths and giggled. Just like in a factory, Dora handed Hannah small stack s of dishes and Hannah handed those stacks to their *tia* who put them in larger stacks on the *sofah*. When they finished, Miriam scrubbed the cabinet clean. She began in the back making sure to catch every crumb before it fell off the shelf.

"*Nána* Hannah," complained her granddaughter Dora, "I am hungry."

"Me too!" chimed in her sister.

Miriam looked down from the ladder over her shoulder, "I am too. Let's stop for a quick lunch. *Mame*, can you serve up the *hornaya* in the dishes on the *sofah*?" And with that, she tucked the rag into her belt and carefully climbed down the ladder.

Her mother nodded an affirmation and took a stack of bowls over to the *hornaya*. On this grate was a pot of boiling potatoes into which the elder Dora stuck a large spoon. Carefully, she put a portion of the traditional snack into each bowl and passed the bowls around. Her namesake followed her with an assortment of spoons and forks.

"Hannah *mio*, is there any salt and pepper?" asked her aunt.

"Salt and pepper?" responded her nieces in mock horror. "Oh *tia*, we ground salt and pepper for hours every night for *Pesah*."

Alejandra smiled knowingly, "Of course you did. That was my job, too. Do you have any for me now?"

"Of course," Hannah, her niece, replied as she passed two bowls filled with spices.

"What do you think we chanted as we ground the spices?" asked Alejandra.

And all the women chanted in unison, "*do Purim a Pesah...mejo ke mi madre no me pariera*." (From Purim to Passover, I wish I'd never had been born.) And they all broke into hysterical laughter.

"Did you grind any for us?" asked their grandmother Dora when the women caught their breath.

"*Si, Nána* Dora," her granddaughter replied.

When the women had finished their repast, Hannah (the younger) gathered the dishes and begrudgingly washed them. Dora (the younger) dried them and restacked them on the *sofah*. As the girls did this, their mother moved the ladder in front of the cabinet where the *losa* were stored.

"Come over here, Alejandra," called Miriam.

Miriam carefully handed down her meat and dairy *losa* to her sister who stacked them on the far end of the *sofah*. When all the dishes were down, Hannah and Dora dutifully took their places in the production line. Then they passed the everyday dishes back to their mother, who put them in the *losa* cabinet for safekeeping. Then she climbed down the ladder, moved it back across the room, and climbed back up and the production line began again with the precious *Pesah* dishes. Finally, Miriam descended the last time from the ladder, wiped her face, with the rag still in her belt, and sat on a chair. Her mother brought her a glass of cold water fresh from the well, while her mother-in-law folded the old cloth on the *sofah* and put it away on her son's bed.

When she returned to the kitchen, she went to the sink and washed her hands; then she turned to her fellow grandmother and said, rather loudly, with her hands on her hips, "Well, *Nána*, it is time we begin our work."

And with that Dora stood up and smiled and went to wash her hands. Then she took one of the unpacked baskets from the corner and started to remove pots of food. Onto the *sofah*, she put pots of *ava fresco, kashkarikas reinvades, tomates reinados, keftes de prasa, juashado or meginah di Pesah, huevos haminados,* and *karne kebab*.

"Hannah, light the stove so we can get this food cooking," commanded Dora a touch too loudly because of her deafness.

So Hannah lit the stove and instructed her granddaughter how to arrange the post in the oven. Then she gathered the jar of freshly chopped nuts the girls had filled, a box of dates, a jug of wine, and a bottle of vinegar. Into a large bowl she poured in some nuts, cut in the dates, and added wine and vinegar and stirred until the mess turned into paste.

"We should have made this yesterday," she commented to herself almost as much as to the others who were puttering around the kitchen.

"You are right," commented her fellow elder, "but sometimes these things just get forgotten in the rush."

"As always, *mia* Dora, you make us all feel better," responded Hannah.

When everything that wasn't kosher for *Pesah* had finally been packed away in the cabinet formerly used of the *losa*, Miriam locked it and handed the key to her eldest daughter.

"Take this down the street to our Turkish neighbors," she commanded. "Sell it for a few coins and remind them we will redeem it in eight days."

Hannah carefully put the key in her pocket solemnly, she nodded her ascent, and quietly left the house.

That evening the extended family gathered around the *sofah* set as a luxurious *sofah*. Hannah and Dora had placed on the started white tablecloth the meat *Pesah* dishes, glasses, silverware, and their mother's and grandmother's silver candlesticks freshly polished. At their father's place and every third chair was a *haggadah*. Moses stood at the head of the table and surveyed his family with pride. The children were dressed in brand new clothes that his mother had made them. His mother, parents-in-law, sister- and brother-in-law, wife, and three youngest children were here. He missed Hiam and David and hoped they had found a home to have *seder* at. That, he realized, was the only imperfection in this evening. Moses tried not to think about the grandchildren that would never be at his *seder*.

Without really listening, Moses heard the women around the *sofah* chant the blessings over the holiday candles. The flicker of these candles and the light from the windows reflected off the embroidered cloth covering the *maztot* he and Alejandro had brought home from the baker's this afternoon and the silver of the *seder* plate. On the *seder* plate were the five symbolic foods: celery, lettuce, boiled egg, lamb shank, and *haroset*.

When the blessing over the candles was complete, Moses lifted his silver cup filled with wine. Everyone at the *sofah* followed his example. At that moment in Rhodes, all over the Mediterranean, in fact all over the worlds, Jews lifted their glasses and recited the *kiddush*. Then they all drank their wine, sat down, and opened their *haggadot*.

XXVI

The following *Shabbat*, the women were seated in the courtyard enjoying the first warm day of spring.

"What did you ever do before the Chief *Rabbi* allowed us to eat rice during *Pesaḥ*?" ask Alejandra.

Her mother answered curtly, "Food was boring. Haven't I said that enough this week?!"

"Oh heavens," responded an exasperated Hannah, "We did not know any better. Everything that contains bread, we would put in the *matzah* crumbs. We even did that substitution for rice."

"But *Pesaḥ* must have been a dull time for food," included Miriam.

"It really was during the War," Dora reminisced. "The ports were closed and food was so expensive. You girls do not remember, but *Padre* and I only ate two meals a day so that you girls had enough to eat. When the Chief *Rabbi* approved rice, we were so excited. That we had in Rhodes, suddenly there was food to eat."

"No," said Miriam, "I guess I never noticed. Maybe *mio hermano* does. I always remember rice."

"Is there rice in America?" asked Alejandra.

"Who knows," responded her mother.

"Miriam will soon enough," her youngest answered.

Dora snapped her head to stare at her elder daughter, "What does your sister mean?"

Miriam looked angrily at her sister. She heaved a deep sigh and then raised her left hand to her face to give herself a moment to gather her thoughts. With her hand over her mouth, she turned to her mother. Miriam's eyes filled with tears.

"*Mame*," she began – her fingers still covering her mouth. "Oh *Mame*," Miriam tried again. "I am sorry. I would tell you. Alejandra should not have said anything."

Her mother stared at her stone faced, "When?"

"*Mame*, when we have settled on a plan."

Dora drew herself up in her chair, so that she sat tall and rigid, "and leaving is not a 'settled plan'?"

Miriam looked at her sister for support, but none was coming. She turned back to her mother.

"*Mame*, we do not know when we are leaving."

"But you are leaving," her mother retorted sternly.

"*Mame*, it is not that business is bad. We have none. We cannot afford both this house and the store." Alejandra opened her mouth to interrupt. Miriam waved her quiet. "*Mame*, we live on what Hiam and David send us. That is not fair to them and it is not fair to the other children. It has been this way for nearly six months."

Tears were slowly rolling down her cheeks as she spoke. Miriam got up from her chair and took the two steps to her mother's. There she did what she had done as a child. She knelt down and laid her head in her mother's lap.

"*Mame*, we have tried. There is no money here. *Hermanio* left for the same reason. Soon, I will have to sell my *maniyas de tchaton*. And then there will be nothing."

The courtyard was silent. It seemed even the birds had hushed themselves. Dora placed one hand on her daughter's head and looked skyward for strength. She could not speak. She knew only tears would come. Alejandra reached out to her mother and took her other hand. And so these women stayed for what seemed forever.

This whole time Hannah hadn't moved, hadn't said a word. What words could she add? This was between a mother and a daughter. Her son would come to her and they would talk. She had suspected something like this was coming. Finances in the house had gotten so tight they could not afford anything but the most modest of necessities. Her friends came less and less for her work. Hannah had not asked why Miriam and Moses were so sad, because she was afraid of the answer.

Hannah sat looking at her hands folded in her lap. Magically water drops appeared on her interlocked thumbs. She didn't realize she was crying until she began to wonder how rain could fall only under her face.

Her world was ending. She had lived through many ends, but they had all also been beginnings. The end of her childhood and living with her parents had been the beginning of living with David and their marriage. The marriage of her youngest son Moses was the end of his childhood, but the beginning of Miriam as her companion. David's death had been the end of their marriage, of her role as a wife, but she could begin again. Caring for her sickly husband had been all consuming. But every one of these had been in the *Juderia* surrounded by family and friends and ancestors. What would she do now? She had lived in this same house since she married David. He had grown up in the house as had his father. Soon her hands were soaked, but she could not move. Where would she go?

The tableau ended with the clatter of a wagon on the cobble stones outside the house. Hannah was shaken free from her thoughts and dried her hands on a handkerchief. Miriam looked up from her mother's lap and saw Hannah looking lost and desolate.

Quickly she rose and went to her mother-in-law. She took Hannah's two gnarled hands and wet handkerchief in her hands.

"*Mia esfuegra*, Moses and I wanted to tell you together," she said gently as she shot her sister an evil look. "We need to talk about this. You are very much part of our concern."

Hannah looked up at her daughter-in-law. All Miriam could see was a frightened, tired, old woman, not the self-confident lady that held the respect of the community. Hannah's eyes were large with fear.

"*Mia ilmuera*, what is to become of me?" asked a tiny voice from this suddenly hopeless face.

Miriam bent over until their eyes were even and they could breathe each other's breath. Her tears fell on that sodden handkerchief.

"That *Mame* is your choice. Could we leave you behind like that old *sofah?* Our children must come with us. Come with us and care for them just as you do here. Or live with any of your other sons or daughters. They all complain we dominate your affections. Spread your love around. A home without you would be incomplete, but we will manage if we must."

Hannah dropped her handkerchief in her lap and raised her hands to cup Miriam's face. A sad smile crept across her face.

"And what of us?" asked Alejandra with forced cheeriness.

Miriam broke the spell with her mother-in-law to face her sister.

"I could not speak to you for telling our secret," she began, which brought a cloud across her sister's face. "But I love you too much. We have discussed this. You and Noah can sell your business and join us in Atlanta. *Mame*, you can come as well. We can all be together."

"No, *Mame*. You and *Padre* stay here with us!" was Alejandra's sharp outburst.

Dora smiled a wry smile and said, "As it always has been, so shall it always be. The two of you must battle over something. I cannot make this decision. It is not mine to make. It is Hiam's. I must talk to him."

At this Alejandra looked at her sister with a smug grin until she saw the ache in her sister's eyes. They all knew that Hiam would never leave his home. It had been his for 200 years.

The banging of the front door and giggles of Dora and Hannah and their friends returning from their afternoon stroll broke the moment. All the women wiped their faces, fixed their dresses, and put on quiet happy faces.

XXVII

That night, after *havadalah*, after the children had gone to bed, Miriam, Moses, and Hannah sat around the *sofah*. Candle bits burned in an assortment of sticks because no candle was too small anymore to burn and a bottle of wine stood on the *sofah*. The silence stretched out among them. It swirled and hung like black smoke.

Finally, Moses began, "*Mame*, we wanted to wait until *Pesah* was over to discuss this with you. We cannot stay. You know we have no money." His voice began to crack, "You know I wish I could stay. With all my heart, I want to stay. But my boys are gone, the boys are leaving. Who will be here to marry *mia fijas*? What can I leave my baby? *Mame*, my life here is no more. I must follow my sons over the sea to work."

The last sentence was barely a whisper. He reached out one hand to Miriam and his other to his mother. They sat in a triangle, clinging to each other.

Now Hannah broke the silence.

She whispered, "You have no choice. There is no work here. You cannot go to the mainland. There is no work there. I know you must go. Over 500 years ago our people came to this island because they were forced to flee Spain because of their religion. Now, we must leave because of money."

"*Mame*, what will you do?" asked her son.

"I can stay here with one of your brothers. They have room; although, the idea of training a new *ilmuera* is not appealing. But none of those homes would be home. I have been in this house since I was nearly 15, that is too many years to count. I cannot bear to see someone else living here. I guess I must go." And while she smiled, they knew her enthusiasm was false.

"Hannah, we can get one of your grandsons to live with you. Daniel's David has just gotten betrothed. He is coming back to live in the *Juderia*. They can move in with you," Miriam replied half-heartedly.

Hannah removed her hands from the circle and sat back, "You are being silly. What young couple, just starting life together wants to live with an old woman like me?"

The couple looked at her in shock.

"*Mame*, we welcomed the chance of you guidance and *Bábu's.*"

"We would have been so lonely without your company. And how could we raise our children without you?" added Miriam.

"*Fijos*, times are different. I could not have imagined living in a house without my in-laws, but I cannot imagine my *inyetos* living with strangers across the sea. However, this is a truth. Daniels' David may have this house, if you wish. To keep it in the family, for him to live in the house his great-grandfather grew-up in would make me happy. I want it to stay in the family, but I finally have Miriam trained the way I want her. When it is time, I will pack my *baoul* and go. *Estamos en galut en Rhodos; estamos en galut* unless we are in Jerusalem. It really does not matter. There, it is decided. Now, I am going to bed." And so Hannah rose with far more bravado than she felt and took a candle to light the way to her bed.

Once she was in her room, she slowly undressed. First to come off was her cap, which she placed on the bed. Then the chains with the *yardan* holding them together she placed on top of her cap, followed by her belt, neatly folded. Hannah slowly removed her *polka de samara*, *antari*, *breshin*, and finally her *chinatian*. Each was carefully folded and stacked upon the last. Then Hannah placed her cap, chains, and belt on the stack. She knelt on the floor in front of her *baoul* and opened it. Gently, she placed her stack of *Shabbat* clothes on top of all the other items in the chest. At that moment, she started to weep. Deep throaty sobs rose from her stomach. Hannah laid her head on her arms and wept.

After 20 minutes, the weeping subsided. Hannah struggled to her feet and found a handkerchief on the table by her bed. Once she had wiped her face and blown her nose, Hannah put on her nightgown and shut her *baoul*. Then she climbed into bed, carefully arranging the covers, and reached for her wedding photograph she kept there.

"*Espozo*, I cannot believe I was ever that young...or thin," she began. "If we were young and you were here, I would feel so much better about this. But to leave everything at my age....Do you remember how we dreamed, when we were first married, of sitting in the courtyard with great-grandchildren at our feet and lemonade in our glasses? That is not to be. I cannot stay here and be a burden to my grandchildren, nor can I go. I never learned Italian when the Italians took Rhodes, how, at my age, will I learn English? Who will I speak to? Not that our *filo* and *ilmuera* are not wonderful, but a gossip with my childhood friends is so..." And Hannah's voice trailed off to silence as she lay in bed thinking of her path. Eventually, she fell asleep clutching the photograph.

XXVIII

Moses, Miriam, and Hannah agreed not to tell the children until *Pesah* was over. So when *Pesah* had ended, and everyone had finished the loaf of bread on the table, Moses called for quiet by banging his hand on the top of the sofah.

"I have something to say to all of you," began Moses with a grave voice. Silence descended on the table and everyone turned their faces to him. "*De la kavesa, fiede el pishkado.* (The head of the family determines the outcome of the family.) And I have come to a decision."

Dora waited in anticipation. Usually, these pronouncements resulted in a family trip to her cousins who lived outside the city, or the redecoration of a room.

Miriam looked at her husband with disgust and shook her head. She knew he was covering his fear and doubt with bravado, but she didn't like that her voice in this matter was being ignored. They had debated, argued, and cried for days over this decision.

The pause lengthened.

Hannah wondered if her father was waiting for effect. She really needed to finish her homework.

"*Mio fiolos,*" Moses continued more gently, "your mother and I have decided we are going to America."

"To visit my brothers? When? For how long?" exploded Alejandro. His brothers had practically become heroes in his mind. It had been so long since he'd seen them that he could barely remember them.

His sisters sat in stunned silence. Under the *sofah*, in secret, they grabbed each others' hand.

"Come here, *mio filo,*" coaxed Miriam, "sit on my lap and calm yourself." Alejandro climbed onto his mohter's lap as directed, but could not calm himself. "We are not going 'for a visit,' *mio filo*. We are going and will come back to Rhodes, someday, for a visit."

"I do not understand," commented a suddenly still Alejandro.

The sisters looked at each other and held on tighter. Neither could decide if this was good or bad news.

"Alejandro, we are going to live in the United States. We are going to be with David and Hiam," added their father.

Alejandro's eyes widened. Then his face grew dark. He jumped off his mother's lap and ran around everyone to his grandmother.

Grabbing her fiercely from behind, he sobbed, "I am not leaving *Nána* Hannah."

His grandmother reached over her head to hug him, "I am going with you. Where else would I go? You are my littlest *inieto*, I have to take care of you."

Alejandro broke into sobs of relief, "But I do not want to leave my friends."

Miriam took a deep breath, "Alejandro and Hannah and Dora, by the time we sell everything we cannot take and settle our debts and say our good-byes school will be out. However, you must do well in school! I am going to take letters from your teachers and from the school master with us. You must show this new country that Rhodelisi are no fools."

"*Mame*," began Hannah hesitantly, "What about *Nána* Dora and *Nóno* David?"

Miriam whispered her response, "They are staying here with your *tiya* and *tiyo*." And then she rose, taking her coffee cup to the sink. It rattled as she walked. "Now, all of you need to finish your homework," she commanded without turning around to look at them.

Hannah and Dora realized that now was no the time to ask more questions. Dora reached for her brother and quietly they went to their bedroom.

The three children dutifully took their books out of their schoolbags. Alejandro sat at the table they used as a desk with his mathematics book. The girls lay on their bed prepared to read. Nothing happened. They could not think.

Dora lay on her back staring at the ceiling.

"Did you know there is a crack in the ceiling? Like a long river. Why have I not noticed it before?" she asked no one.

"What crack?" Alejandro asked, anxious to be involved in any conversation, looking at the ceiling.

"Right there," his sister answered pointing to it.

"What does a stupid crack have to do with anything?" Hannah interrupted. "What does anything mean?!" she cried as she threw her book across the room.

"Hannah! You have been jealous of Sarah ever since she said she was going to America to be with her *hermanio* and *despaozado*, now you get to go. Now we can be with our *hermanio!*" Dora responded with exasperation.

"Oh, what do you know," Hannah growled. "*Naná* Dora and *Nóno* Hiam will not come. And what about *Tiya* Alejandra and *Tiyo* Noah? Hiam and David left and never came back. Neither will we. Have you thought of that?"

"We are not coming back?" asked their little brother. "Then who will collect our mail from Pasha?"

"Silly boy, Yacov Israel's daughters will not announce our names when the mail is delivered. We will not have mail here any more. Our mail will come to our home in America. Besides who sends us mail?" answered a frustrated Hannah.

"*Hermanio!*"

"Right, and we will be living with him."

"But Hannah," interrupted Dora, "what about the letters from *Mame's hermanio?*"

"Oh," she responded off hand, "*Mame* will write to him and let him know where we are." He had left so long ago that Hannah and Dora barely remembered him. Mostly, he was only a series of stories that their mother, aunt, and grandparents shared with them.

Alejandro pondered what his sisters had said and then broke out in tears, "What about Antonio?"

Not quite understanding his question, Dora curtly responded, "He will stay here with his parents. His father's job pays well, I am sure."

This only made Alejandro cry more. Hannah and Dora looked at each other in confusion. Then, at almost the same moment, it occurred to them what was troubling Alejandro. Hannah motioned Alejandro over to their bed with her hand. He climbed in between them, still sobbing.

His oldest sister put her arm protectively around him and gently whispered, "We are going on a grand adventure and poor Antonio must stay here with his parents and go to the same old boring school and do the same old boring things."

"But," Alexander pushed out between sobs, "he is…my…best friend."

Dora smiled, although she was now almost in tears, "Then you will be like *hermanio* and David and write him about our travels. And then, when he is older, he can come and visit us."

"Do you think," panted Alejandro, "*Bábu* will let him stay?"

"Of course," answered Hannah. "Now, we heard *Mame*. We have to show those Americans we are not fools. Time for homework."

Alejandro crawled out of his sisters' bed and went back to the table, where he wiped his face on his shirt tails. Then he looked back at his sisters mournfully.

"Okay, silly," said Dora, "you can climb in, too. But this time – take off your shoes."

So Alejandro kicked off his shoes and snuggled in between his sisters, laying on his stomach with his math textbook propped on a pillow. When their parents came into the room later to check homework and get everyone ready for bed, they found their three children asleep, arms entangled. Gently, they removed books from the mess and piled them quietly on the table. Then they took the blanket off Alejandro's bed and lay it over the three and silently left the room.

XXIX

It did not take long for news of the family's leaving to travel around the *Juderia*. It was a relatively small community of only a few thousand people. Moses' decision to depart was not uncommon, though taking his family was. While some families had left, it was still more common for only men to go. However, no one was really surprised. Money was scarce.

Despite the bad economy, it had taken only two weeks for Moses and Miriam to sell every item from the store. Then they sold the store itself and walked home quietly. They sat in the courtyard, holding hands, with glasses of untouched lemonade on the table between them.

Hannah had decided the best thing to do was to leave them alone, so she went to visit a friend. She had been doing a lot of that since she had decided to go. It was almost like she knew she was dying. She traded keepsakes, scarves, photographs, and recipes with the women she had spent almost her entire life with. Every visit was both exhilarating and exhausting. Exhilarating to relive wonderful times and exhausting to always seem positive and excited about her new adventure, which seemed far more a burden than a gift.

When the children came home from school, they ran into the kitchen, as they always did, to have some treat their grandmother had prepared and share their day with her. But they stopped short, she wasn't there. They dropped their book bags, and ran into the courtyard. Sometimes, on nice days like today, she would be in the courtyard playing cards with friends. Hannah stopped first; Dora bumped into her; and Alejandro slammed into Dora. Then he shoved his way between his sisters to see what had made them stop.

In the courtyard sat their parents, holding hands, the lemonade untouched on a small table between them. They didn't say a word. They simply stared at the cobbles at their feet.

The children were silent. They had never seen their parents holding hands. On rare occasions, they might touch each other, but never hold hands. As modern as their parents were, they never broke the rules of behavior.

Alejandro pulled on the back of Hannah's blouse. She looked down at him and he looked up quizzically. She chewed the inside of her cheek for a moment and then reached out to Dora. The sisters needed only one glance to know what to do. Hannah looked back down at Alejandro, put one finger over her lips to quiet him, and then they backed into the house. Silently, they returned to the kitchen and retrieved their book bags.

"Come," commanded Hannah in whisper, "we will go to *Nána* Dora's."

Quickly and quietly they left.

Once outside Alejandro could contain himself no longer, "That was strange. Why are *Mame* and *Bábu* acting so different? Did *Nána* Hannah die?"

His sisters didn't answer, so he repeated his question even louder, "Did *Nána* Hannah die?!"

"What? No, silly," answered Dora.

"How do *you* know?" asked her little brother.

"Simple," responded Hannah. "Had she died someone would have come to get us from school early and the *Bikur Holim* would be would be in the house preparing *Nána* Hannah and the house for a funeral."

"Oh," responded Alejandro. "So what did happen?"

"I have no idea," snapped Hannah.

And the conversation ended as they entered Dora and Hiam's home. There they found their grandmother cleaning from the afternoon meal. They hadn't knocked before they came in because they'd forgotten. Usually, they knocked and entered before being welcomed. This time they startled their grandmother who dropped a pot on the floor. The loud crash brought their grandfather into the room.

"What is the matter children? You startled me! Sit down, let me get you something to eat," chattered their grandmother without taking a breath as she leaned down to pick up her post.

"*Vos, espoza* these children look disturbed. Be quiet and let them speak," commanded their grandfather.

Alejandro immediately began with a muddle of ideas," It is all wrong. *Mame* and *Bábu* are holding hands. And Dora says *Nána* Hannah is not dead. But she was not home. And the lemonade was full."

Nóno Hiam looked at his grandson with a mixture of confusion, amusement, and concern. He sat down in a chair and motioned the boy over to him.

Putting an arm gently around his youngest grandson, he turned to his granddaughters, "*Inietas*, now carefully, slowly tell me the whole story."

Hannah drew a breath, "*Nóno*, we came home from school…"

Here Dora interrupted, "Like we do every school day."

"Yes, the same as every day. And went in to the kitchen to greet *Nána* Hannah."

"Like we do everyday," came the interruption from Dora.

Hannah gave her sister a dirty look and continued, "But *Nána* Hannah was not there. The house was quiet. So,…"

"So we went into the courtyard and there were *Mame* and *Bábu*. That is what is so odd," finished Dora in one breath.

"Dora, let me finish!" reprimanded the older sister. "So we went in to the courtyard and there were *Mame* and *Bábu*. They were sitting, holding hands, staring at the floor, not speaking."

"And they had not drunk their lemonade," added Alejandro.

"We had no idea what to do, so we came here," finished Hannah.

Hiam looked at his wife, who had stopped bustling around the kitchen while the children told their story. She nodded at him and he nodded at her.

"*Inyetos*, let me get you some fruit," *Nána* Dora said as she put a basket of fruit on one arm and a pile of plates and glasses in one hand, with a pitcher of water in the other. Then she put everything on the *sofah* and drew up a chair.

Haim blew a large lungful of air out of his mouth and paused, "I guess your parents did not tell you."

"Tell us what?" the three asked expectantly.

"Today, they sold the store."

"Why?" asked Alejandro.

"*Mio inieto*, you cannot take the store with you when you go. Your *bábu* has sold everything in the store and finally the shop itself. Now," his grandfather added, "They have nothing left. They only have money, which," and here he tried to sound positive, "you need to buy your tickets and food to get to America."

Hannah and Dora put down their snacks simultaneously.

"I guess," began Hannah, "I had not thought about that. I mean I knew they could not take the shop; I just had not realized they would have to sell it."

Nána Dora stated quietly, "It is very hard for them. Your *padre* worked in that shop with his father. Your mother and I went to that shop after the matchmaker had suggested your *bábu* as a match. Your parents worked there and thought they would until one of you took it over. It was their life and now they have to find a new one."

Some tears trickled down her face. She hastily wiped them on her sleeve, so the children wouldn't see them.

"Are *Mame* and *Bábu* going to have a store in America?" Alejandro asked innocently.

"I hope so," answered his grandfather, "but we do not know. It will be your job to write to me and tell me all about what your parents do. And," here his voice cracked, "what you do." And he pulled his youngest grandson close to hold him and buried his face in Alejandro's coat.

"*Nóno*, why not come too?" asked Alejandro. "Come and visit."

"*Mio inieto*, I am too old and tired to take such a journey and your *nána* could never decide what to pack and what to leave. *Mio inieto*, these things are for the young," came David's muffled reply.

Alejandro could not let this go, "So why is *Nána* Hannah coming? She is older than you?!"

"Alejandro, you *must* be quiet," reprimanded Dora. "You cannot speak to our *nóno* that way."

"Dora, it is quite alright. Sometimes, we need answers," remarked their grandmother. "*Nána* Hannah has decided to go because she takes care of you and is afraid there will be no one in America to take care of you. We have decided to stay so that there will be someone to help *Tiya* Alejandra and *Tiyo* Noah when their baby comes."

The three children looked up expectantly and asked in unison, "They are having a baby?"

"No, *inyetos*, not yet, but someday," replied their grandmother sadly.

There were a few minutes of absolute silence in the room as everyone contemplated the situation.

Eventually, Hannah looked at her grandmother and whispered, "That means we might never see you again." Tears began to run down her face. "Oh *Nána* that is so unfair," she cried and threw herself on the floor at her grandmothers' feet, wrapping her arms around her grandmother's waist. She looked very much the same as her mother had when Dora discovered they were leaving.

Dora stroked her granddaughter's head. Dora came behind her grandmother and encircled her neck with her arms and placed her cheek on the top of her grandmother's head, tears running down her face. Alejandro clung to his grandfather as Hiam clutched his grandson. No one spoke. No one could speak. All that was heard was an occasional sniffle.

Quite a while later, maybe 10 minutes, maybe 20, Alejandra entered the room and encountered this vignette. It was very much, had it been darker in the room, like a family scene by a Dutch master, but Alejandra didn't know this; she'd never been to an art museum. She stood in the doorway for awhile absorbing the poignant scene. If everyone hadn't been so sad, she would have enjoyed it.

With a forced cheeriness, Alejandra shattered the moment, "Why haven't I gotten a hug? Am I not special enough?"

The three children with tear streamed faces released their holds on their grandparents and flung themselves at their favorite aunt. They rushed her with such force that she almost fell and had to steady herself on the doorframe before grabbing them in her arms.

"Oh *Tiya*," sobbed Dora. "I do not want to leave you."

"Hush *mio nina*," whispered Alejandra through kisses and tears. "We will always be together again. We are always together in our hearts."

"Promise," sobbed Hannah.

"Promise what?" asked Alejandra, holding on even tighter.

"Promise you will take good care of *mio nána* and *nóno*," said Hannah.

That made their grandmother laugh, "oh, *mio inieta* I am staying here to take care of your *tiya* not the other way around."

But Hannah and Alejandra knew the truth and Alejandra whispered directly in her niece's ear so no one else would hear, "I promise."

Then she said in a loud voice, "All right, enough tears. This is not a funeral; this is the beginning of an adventure. You have some serious responsibilities to manage."

Her nephew looked up at her wiping his face on his sleeve and inquired, "What responsibilities?"

"*Si, Tiya*, what are we supposed to do" asked Dora wiping her face on her aunt's coat.

"Well...," thought Alejandra, "since I am not so lucky as to go, you must write every week and tell us everything. What you did. What it looks like. What new things you learned."

"Yes, yes," Hannah interrupted, "Everyone says that."

Alejandra gave her elder niece a haughty look, "Did I finish? *Gracias.*" She gave her full attention to Hannah, "You must take care of your *mame*. She is my sister and I will not be there to help and give a hug, so you must be extra good and tell me about how your *mame* is." Then she turned to Dora, "You, *mio nina*, must continue your practice of reporting on your brother. Your parents do not know half of the mischief he makes but" and here she turned an evil eye on Alejandro, "I do. I can manage him no matter how far away you are."

"What about me?" piped in Alejandro. "I deserve a special job."

"So you do, the most special one of all. You must make sure to give your sisters and your *mame* and *bábu* and *nána* an extra hug every day and remind them it is from me," and Alejandra kissed the top of her nephew's head to stop her tears.

"Awww," whined Alejandro, "hugs?"

His grandmother smiled, "Si, *inieto*, hugs. You know how much those hugs help you heal, give you strength, so you must pass that along."

"Now *inyetos*," interrupted Hiam. "I am sure your other *nána* is looking for you. Take your bags and hurry home. Do not upset your parents tonight. Do your homework and your chores like good children."

Hannah, Dora, and Alejandro wiped their faces on and blew their noses in their handkerchiefs, collected their bags, and quietly left the house. As they got to the door, Noah appeared. Each child sadly hugged their uncle as they left. Not a word was spoken.

Noah walked into the room with a befuddled look on his face, "What is with those children? Did someone die?"

Alejandra took his hand and looked at him mournfully. "No,...yes, ...no. They just realized what they are leaving behind."

XXX

No one in the house really spoke about what was going on. They all came on their own in their own time to the realization that talking did nothing. Each still had their moments of excitement at the adventure, sadness at leaving behind very precious memories and people, and ambivalence about the entire situation.

Tension, however, was high in the house. While the children still attended school, Moses and Miriam had nothing to do. Moses spent his mornings with the older men at each other's homes, just not his, talking politics, drinking coffee, and playing backgammon.

Miriam would stay home to help Hannah until her mother-in-law could no longer stand her daughter-in-law hovering about and would send her to her mother's. Sometimes Miriam would go to her mother's, sometimes she would go to her sister's shop and help there or sit and chat with her sister and the customers.

For Miriam, Moses, and Hannah it had become a time of waiting. They were waiting for additional funds from the boys in America. They were waiting for their children in school to take their exams. They were waiting for the departure of their ship.

Miriam and Hannah had debated and argued over what items to take and what to leave behind for Hannah's grandson and his new wife.

"*Esfuegia*, we must be careful what we take," began every conversation. "It must fit into our *baouls* or the trunks." Moses had determined the best way to pack was for each person to have one trunk and one bag they could easily carry. That way the chance of their belongings surviving the trip would be greater.

"Si, *mio ilmuera*," was always Hannah's reply. "But you only have half a lifetime to choose from, I have my entire lifetime. How can I decide? Every plate, every spoon carries a memory." At which point she would break down in tears.

However, there were certain family heirlooms that both women agreed would go. Their silver candlesticks were a must, and, of course, they were small and light. Moses' silver *kiddush* cup also had to go. Moses' *siddur*, and the family *tanakh*, and *haggadah* there was no debate about. They had both decided individually to bring their *baouls*. Miriam had hopes that their *baouls* would fit inside a trunk, so they could pack even more. So everything in their *baouls*, their entire dowries, was going with them. Neither woman could imagine going without their hope chests.

The two had a serious debate about the family photographs. Hannah wanted to bring all these people, her parents and grandparents, aunts and uncles, with her. Miriam wanted to take them as well, but could not imagine filling a trunk with just pictures. After a few days of arguing and picking over the pictures, they decided to take the photographs out of the frames and cut the pages out of the photo album. That way, every photo could be packed.

Deciding on the rest of the household items was nearly impossible. An entire household was going to be established in America, but what could they find and what wouldn't they? How much could they afford to replace?

"You should have asked David and Hiam when we had first decided," was Moses' exasperated reply when asked his opinion.

"What does a man know about setting up a home?" his mother snapped back crossly.

"That *Mame* is exactly the point. My needs are simple: my clothes, my *tallit*, my *tanakh*, and *kiddush* cup. You women can argue about the rest," was the last comment Moses would make on the debate.

Finally, they agreed on the *haminero* and dismantled it, their silver *Pesaḥ* cutlery, their good *Pesaḥ* dishes, the children's favorite books – there was no way Alejandro was leaving without his Christmas gift from his best friend Antionio. Each woman had a secret hope that there would be extra space for some other items.

One day a *hamale* arrived at the door with a cart full of trunks. Hannah and Miriam stood in the doorway in shock. The *hamale* handed them an envelope and asked them to step aside.

"I was told to put them inside the house," he announced in Greek. The women stood to one side.

"What does the message say?" asked Hannah anxiously.

"Here in the street?" responded Miriam.

"Just tell me," sighed her mother-in-law.

"Fine," responded her daughter-in-law. "It reads: We wanted to send you on your way in style. Your *boauls* should fit nicely. Our love, *Mame*, *Bàbu*, Alejandra, and Noah."

"Three, four, five," counted Hannah.

"Five what?"

"Six. They bought each of us a new trunk!" exclaimed Hannah in shock.

The *hamale* came out after dropping the last one in the last one in the house and Miriam reached into her apron pocket for a coin to tip him.

"Oh no, I have been paid in full. I was told to accept no tip," was his refusal as he grabbed the handles of the cart and disappeared around the corner.

The two women wandered into their house and stared at the six steamer trunks that filled their living room.

"They will fit our *baouls*," said Miriam in wonder as tears filled her eyes.

Hannah's hand gripped hers.

"You have a generous family," she commented.

Miriam whispered, "They are as much yours as you are mine."

XXXI

"*Mame, Nána!* It is over!" screamed Alejandro as he stormed into the house. His grandmother smiled warmly at her grandson.

"*Nána*, we are going to the beach to meet some friends to celebrate," added Hannah. "If that is ok," she added quickly.

"We thought you would," said their mother. "So here is a basket of lemonade, and water, pita, feta, and olives. Take the blanket. Have some fun and be back by dusk."

"*Mame, gracias.* You know everything," Dora squealed as she grabbed her mother in a tight hug.

"I went to school too, and I remember the pleasure of the last day of school. We always went to the beach," their mother reminisced. "Just be careful and be back by dusk."

"And please change your clothes," added their grandmother.

The children dropped their bags where they stood in the kitchen and ran to their room.

"Alejandro, go away," Miriam and her mother-in-law heard the girls' command their brother. Then they heard him run down the hall to his grandmother's room. When the three children returned to the kitchen, they had on bathing suits under their play clothes.

"*Gracias, Nána. Gracias, Mame,*" the three said in unison.

"*Mame*, I promise to bring them both home by dusk," Hannah said suddenly mature.

"Go have fun," commanded their mother. And they left quickly and noisily.

"Oh, *Esfuegra*, I remember the sweetness of the last day of school. The hope of the summer and the freshness of watermelon," Miriam commented wistfully. "There are times, like now, I miss being a child."

"Dear Miriam," Dora said sadly, "I miss being married. I miss being just wed. And yes, I miss being a child."

"Well, *Esfuegra*, they should enjoy childhood as long as they can. These friends they have only a few weeks left with. They need these memories of the *Juderia*."

XXXII

After the *motzi*, led by Hiam as patriarch, silence reigned. The only noise one could hear was the scraping of knives against plates and slurping from glasses. The meal consisted of favorites: Hannah's *macaronia* and Alejandro's *huevos haminados*, Dora's *reshikas* and Miriam's olives, for Mordechai his favorite wine and his mother's *halvah*. Anyone else would have thought this an odd menu, but Hannah and Alejandra wanted everyone to have their treat, no matter what the expense. The two had saved and horded for over a month and would scrimp and scrape food for another month. However, for their last dinner in the *Juderia* this mother and daughter would spare no expense to show their love for the people they loved so deeply.

As much as they felt the excitement of the adventure, none of those leaving could express the overwhelming sadness they felt at leaving could express the overwhelming sadness they felt at leaving the *Juderia*; their home for centuries. This is what kept the six silent. They could not imagine life without Hannah, Hiam, Alejandra, and Noah, nor could the four staying behind imagine life without these six.

When the meal was over, no one moved. No dish was carried to the sink. That simple action would mean the meal was over and the time to meet the ferry to leave was that much closer.

"Namesake, you are quieter than a mouse," Alejandro said trying to joke and break the heavy silence.

Alejandro ran from his chair to his grandfather and climbed into his lap. There the two sat, arms wrapped around each other, weeping. Hiam had sent his older grandsons away, but they were men; they had become *b'nai mitzvah*. Alejandro would become a bar mitzvah far from the synagogue his ancestors had prayed in for generations. Everyone at the table saw Hiam weeping, but they could not understand the depth of his sorry. Alejandro just wept because he knew he'd miss his grandfather – the man who spoiled him and loved him no matter what mischief he got into.

The sight of these two, the man and the child, weeping uncontrollably, was unbearable to everyone else. With tear streaming down their faces, Dora, Hannah, and Miriam threw themselves on the elder Hannah and Alejandra wrapped herself around them.

"*Mia ninas*," cooed the elder Hannah. She desperately wanted to share some important secrets with them, but her sorrow was so deep she could think of nothing.

Moses felt the tears in his eyes and tried to rise from his chair, but his legs would not support him.

He held his head in his hands and moaned, "What have I done? Is this the right thing to do?"

His mother stood up and put her arms around him.

"*Mio fijo*, what do you mean? You have made the best decision for the future," whispered Dora in her son's ear. "It may be hard now, but on what would you feed your children? Where would you find the money?"

"Oh, *Mame*," he wept, "how can I hurt my wife so much?" He turned to his mother, "What of you? Stay here. Be buried with *Bábu*."

"*Mio fijo*, I cannot stay here to die. There are times to rest and times to go on an adventure. Your father and I will find each other again, when I am gone, it does not matter where my body is buried." And here she smiled a wan smile, "besides, I have trained your wife to be the perfect daughter-in-law, why would I stay behind and have ato start again."

Moses gave a weak laugh and clung to his mother, just as his son clung to his grandfather.

Finally, Noah could endure no more, "Is this the way we send people on a trip with weeping and moaning? I do not think so. The children of Israel crossed a sea and celebrated, so we should celebrate before you leave. *Ye-hi ratson mil'fa-ne-cha Adonai elo-hei-nu vei-lo-hei avo-teinu sheh-toli-cheinu l'shalom v'ta-tzi-deinu l'shalom, v'tad-ri-cheinu l'shalom v'ta-gi-einu lim-choz chef-tseinu l'chayim ul-simcha ul-shalom. V'ta-tsi-leinu mikaf kol oyeiv v'oreiv v'listim v'cha-yot ra-ot ba-derech u-mikol mi-nei fur-a-niyot ha-mit-ragshot lavo la-olam. V'tish-lach b'racha b'chol ma-asei ya-deinu.v'tit-neinu l'chein ul-chesed ul-racha-mim be'ei-necha uv-einei chol ro-einu, v'tishma kol tacha-nu-neinu. Ki Eil sho-mei-a t'fi-lah v'ta-cha-nun a-tah. Ba-ruch a-tah Adonai sho-mei-a t'fi-lah.*" (May it be Your will, Eternal One, Beloved of our ancestors, to lead us in peace and direct our steps in peace; to guide us in peace, to support us in peace and to bring us to our destination in life, joy and peace. Deliver us from the hands of every enemy and lurking foe, and robbers and wild beasts on the journey, and from all kinds of calamities that may come to and afflict the world; and bestow blessing upon all our actions. Grant me grace, kindness and mercy in Your eyes and in the eyes of all who behold us, and bestow bountiful kindness upon us. Hear the voice of my prayer, for You hear everyone's prayer. Blessed are You Lord, who hears prayer.)

This prayer brought everyone out of their despair and they stood up and held hands in a big circle. They all felt that if they let go, the family would fall apart.

Hiam raised his head and recited, "*Yivarechecha Adonai viyishmirecha. Ya'er Adonai panav elecha veechuneka. Yeesa Adonai panav elecha viyasem lecha shalom.*" (May G-d bless you and guard you. May G-d shine His countenance upon you and be gracious to you. May G-d turn His countenance toward you and grant you peace.)

With that the family felt they could tear themselves apart.

Moses gave Hiam a bear hug and Hiam whispered in his son-in-law's ear, "I gave to you *mio niña* to care for. Remember she is still *mio niña* no matter how far you two travel."

"She is precious to me as well," responded Moses. Then he broke the hug and walked to the door. Each of his family hugged Noah, Alejandra, Dora, and finally Hiam. In silence, this receiving line worked. Once the hugs were done, Moses and his family walked the dusky street home. They did not turn back and wave.

XXXIII

In the morning, the family, which had remained quiet through the night, rose and gathered in the kitchen. They were still quiet. With as few words as possible they ate breakfast.

Miriam was the first to speak, "Hannah, please help your *Nána* wash the dishes. Dora please make all the beds and make sure every room is neat so when your cousin arrives everything is ready for them. *Mio fijo*, you can help your *Bábu* and me lock the trunks." Slowly she rose from the table and made her way to the front room where the new trunks were waiting.

No one dared question Miriam's authority. Miriam and her mother-in-law had agreed that anything they were not taking they would leave for Dora's grandson and his new wife as a wedding gift. So after Hannah and her grandmother washed the dishes, they put them away, and scrubbed the kitchen as if it were the week before *Pesach*. Dora made each bed as if it were just before *Shabbat* and shook the rag rugs and swept the floor.

Then the three of them met up in the front room where Moses, Miriam, and Alejandro were just locking the trunks. Without a word, when the trunks were all locked Moses handed Miriam a set of keys and put the others in his pocket. At that moment, there was a knock on the door. Two *hamales* came in and loaded the trunks onto their carts. The children and two women followed the *hamales* out the door. Moses took one last look around the room and then shut the door behind him.

Miriam had insisted no one walk them to the harbor and no one send them off. They had spent the week saying their goodbyes. At the harbor they met Hannah's friend Sarah who was travelling with them. Moses had agreed to take Sarah along with his family and deliver her to her *hermanio*, since they were all going to Montgomery. As soon as Hannah saw her friend, she called out her name.

Miriam grabbed her daughter's arm, "Hush! I know you consider this a great adventure and you are excited to travel with your best friend, but remember Sarah is leaving her parents. Let them have their time together."

"Oh, *Mame*. I forgot that part," was a subdued Hannah's response.

When Sarah finally separated herself from her parents, and joined Moses' family, Hannah put her arm gently around her best friend. Dora quietly took Sarah's hand.

Sarah's father took Moses aside, "*Gracias*, Moses. I feel better knowing *mia niña* is traveling with you. A girl should not travel alone."

Moses put his hand on his friend's shoulder, "She will be one of my daughters."

"Here are Sarah's papers and a letter for her *hermanio. Gracias*," said the father weeping. He could contain himself no longer and turned away from the harbor.

Then the seven *Rhodelisi* boarded the ferry to Naples where they would meet the S.S. Saturnia and head towards the New World. Their new world.

Epilogue

Miriam sat in the women's section of *Or Ve Shalom* clutching two letters in her hand. Miraculously, they had arrived the same week. In the *Juderia*, she had really only gone to the synagogue for the holidays; here in Atlanta, she had started coming at least once a month outside of holidays. Partially, it was the comfort. At least at the synagogue she felt more of a *Rhodelisi*. At the synagogue, *Ladino* was spoken and people were familiar.

She was here early to be alone. The two letters were crushed together in her left hand so that they seemed almost one. Slowly, the tears started to roll down her cheeks. Miriam had desperately tried not to cry because she knew once she stared it wouldn't end. In her heart, she spoke to G-d. Her emotions were too powerful to even make her lips move.

"Why? Why have you done this? How could you do this?" And now the tears poured from her eyes turning her face into a wadi. She wiped her face with the handkerchief in her right hand as she stared at the letters in her left. And then she whispered, "*Gracias, mio dieo.*"

She really didn't know which emotion she was crying with. One letter was over six months old. It had taken six months to travel from the Holy Land to her. It was the first letter she had received from her sister since 1938. It wasn't a long letter. Miriam didn't care – the entire story could be told later, if any one cared. This was all she needed to ease her heart. Her sister Alejandra and brother-in-law Noah and Noah's two nephews and three nieces were safe in the Holy Land. Her sister was safe and alive. Even though she was sad for those five children, she was happy as well. Alejandra and Noah had the joy of raising children, and the knowledge that these children were safe. The families, the people, would continue on. She would write her sister on Sunday, when *Shabbat* was over and tell her the news: of their grandchildren, of school graduations, of their success in business. But mostly of the joy she felt knowing her sister was alive and well. Maybe she would send some money, as well. Then she would write to her brother and tell him. The other letter had been long awaited. While the first was a welcome surprise, the arrival of the second had been awaited with much trepidation. As soon as the Red Cross had announced at the end of the war that they were reconnecting families, Miriam had written, searching for everyone they had left behind. There hadn't been news since 1944. She had read the news reports, seen the news reels, and heard the rumors. Only last month, the three survivors the synagogue had sponsored had moved away. They had returned to Rhodes after the war, but could not stay. It was too painful, too lonely.

Even after hearing their stories, Miriam had held out hope. There had been no news for over three years. And the letter had come. Not a soul was left. None of Moses' brothers or sisters or their children lived. None of their cousins lived. The tears began again. There was no hope now. Miriam wept uncontrollably.

She wept for her beloved mother-in-law who had endured being a stranger in a strange land, so her family could be better off. But Hannah had died without knowing what had happened to her other children; those who had remained behind. Miriam could not decide if Hannah was better off not knowing or if she would have been more content with the knowledge. There was no answer. Hannah knew now. Hannah had known since her soul had returned to *Adonai*. Hannah had known long before they had.

And Miriam wept. Miriam wept for the horrors her family had endured before they died. Miriam wept for the destruction of her world. The *Juderia* was now only a memory. And she wept because her sister and brother were alive and safe and she and her family were alive and safe and prosperous. Some day, some how, they would all be together again.

GLOSSARY

Adonai – Hebrew meaning "Lord," in reference to G-d

Anteri – a coat-like dress of heavy silk or velvet with slits up to the waist worn on special occasions by traditional Sephardic women

Ava fresca – fava beans

Avrit – Hebrew meaning "the afternoon prayer service"

Bábu – Ladino meaning "father," used by children

Baklava – a Mediterranean dessert made of filo, nuts, cinnamon, and a honey or sugar syrup

Baoul – Ladino meaning "hope chest," a trunk into which girls and married women stored their dowry

Bar mitzvah – Hebrew meaning "son of the commandments," used to refer to a boy who at the age of 13 leads the Sabbath service for the first time

Besorot Tovot – Hebrew meaning "good news"

Bikur Holem – burial society

B'nai mitzvah – (P.) see *bar mitzvah*

Bourekas – a desert made of fried dough and topped with honey or sugar syrup

Breshin – a sheath or tunic of gauze-like material slit up to the waist worn on special occasions by traditional Sephardic women

Brit milah – Hebrew meaning covenant of circumcision

Brit milot – (P.) see *brit milah*

Burmeulos – Ladino Hanukah treat, a deep fried fritter

Calle Ancha – Spanish meaning "Broad Street," a specific street still found in the city of Rhodes

Cenci – Italian meaning "scraps of fabric," an Epiphany treat of deep fried dough dusted with sugar

Ceppo – a triangular structure with 3 or 4 shelves, only about 3 feet high

Chinatian – a kind of pantaloon worn by traditional Sephardi women as part of their everyday dress

Collegio Rabbinico Couvitto – Italian meaning "Rabbinic College" founded originally in 1829 in Padua

Desayano de keso – filo dough filled with cheese

Despaozado – Ladino meaning "fiancé"

Dieo – Ladino meaning "G-d"

Dishabille – a wide lace blouse worn by more modern Rhodelisi

Dulce de lemon – candied lemon peel

Dulce de portokal – candied orange peel

El – Ladino meaning "he" in the 3rd person singular form, often used to refer to one's husband

En Koyamar – Ladino meaning "G-d forbid"

Ermana – Ladino meaning "sister"

Esfuegra – Ladino meaning "mother-in-law"

Esfuegro – Ladino meaning "father-in-law"

Esklava de amor – title of a Rhodelisi song, in English "A slave of love"

Espoza – Ladino meaning "wife"

Espozo – Ladino meaning "husband"

Estamos en galut en Rhodos – Ladino meaning "We are exile in Rhodes"

Fija – Ladino meaning "daughter"

Fijás – (P.) see *fija*

Fijo – Ladino meaning "son"

Fullar – hardboiled egg covered with strips of dough

Ginevra – a thermos like container made of pottery

Gracias – Spanish meaning "thank you"

Grazie – Italian meaning "thank you"

Güestro – Ladino meaning "your"

Guerta de los Limones – Ladino meaning "Garden of the Lemons"

Habarim Buenos…di los alishados – Ladino meaning "good news from far away"

Hag Purim – Hebrew meaning "Happy Purim"

Haggadah – Hebrew meaning "telling," the text used during the *seder* ceremony

Haggadot – (P.) see *Haggadah*

Halvah – sweet treat made from ground sesame seeds and either sugar or honey syrup. Often nuts or dried fruit are added.

Hamale – a porter or errand boy, either Greek, Jewish, or Turkish

Hamets – leavened food forbidden during *Pesach*

Haminero – a tin container originally for kerosene that was reshaped to become a cook stove

Hanukah – the eight day winter celebration of the Jewish defeat over the Greeks in 168 B.C.E.

Hanukiah – the nine cupped menorah designed for use during the eight day celebration of Hanukah

Haroset – a mixture of nuts, fruit, and wine eaten during the Pesach ceremonial meal to represent the mortar the Hebrews used in building the Egyptian pyramids

Havdalah – from the Hebrew meaning to separate or divide, this ceremony separates the holy day of Shabbat from the common days of the week

Havdalah candle – a special braided candle with four strands used during the *havdalah* ceremony. Each strand represents different types of Jews.

Hazan – the chanter and leader of the synagogue service

Hermano – Ladino meaning "brother," used only in reference to the eldest son in the family

Hornaya – charcoal grate

Huevos haminados – Spanish for eggs from the *haminados*. They are eggs slow cooked for 5-6 hours in onion skins, vinegar, olive oil, and sometimes tea leaves or coffee grounds

Ibrik – Greek term for the pot in which Turkish coffee is made

Ilmuera – Ladino meaning "daughter-in-law"

Inieta – Ladino meaning "granddaughter"

Inieto – Ladino meaning "grandson"

Inyetos – Ladino meaning "grandchildren"

Juderia – The Jewish quarter of the city of Rhodes.

Kahal – Hebrew meaning "community" or "congregation," the Sephardim use this word instead of synagogue

Kahal Kadosh Shalom – Hebrew meaning "Holy Congregation of Peace," the oldest synagogue in Greece and the only remaining on the island of Rhodes after the Second World War

Kal de Shalom – Ladino meaning "Community of Peace," a synagogue in the *Juderea*

Kaltiamiro – Ladino for the ceremony of searching for the *hamets*

Karne kebab – beef stewed in its own juice

Kashkarikas reinvades – fava bean shells stuffed with ground meat

Kashrut – Hebrew meaning "keeping kosher"

Kaveh – Ladino meaning "coffee"

Keftes de prasa – leek patties

Kiddush – the prayer said over the wine before the meal

Kosher – Term describing a manner of handling food and determining foods allowed to be eaten by Jewish law. In brief, animals must be killed in a humane way and all the blood removed, of water creatures only scaled fish may be eaten, and meat and dairy projects kept separate.

Kuashado di spinaka – spinach soufflé

Ladino – language spoken by Sephardic Jews. It is written with Hebrew characters and includes Greek, Turkish, Arabic, and French words depending upon the speaker's country of origin.

La Allianca – Italian, a slang reference to L'Alliance Israélite Universelle

L'Alliance Israélite Universelle – French meaning The Universal Israeli Alliance. A system of schools around the world founded by Baron de Rothschild to educate Jewish children.

La Befana – the witch that Italian children believe brings them their Epiphany gifts

La Fiesta de Purim – Ladino meaning "The Festival of Purim"

La Kay Ancha – Ladino meaning "The Wide Way," the name of one of the streets in the Juderia

Lira – unit of Italian money

Losa – Spanish meaning "pottery," the term used to refer to the *Pesach* dishes

Maestro espaniol – Ladino meaning "our Spanish," implying Ladino

Makaron Reinda – meat and macaroni casserole

Mame – Ladino meaning "Mother" or "Mamma," specifically used by the Greek Sephardim

Maniyas de tchaton – wide gold bracelets

Megillah – Hebrew meaning "scroll" or "book"

Megillat Esther – Hebrew meaning "Book of Esther," the story read on Purim

    Minyan – the required 10 adult men needed to hold a public prayer service

Mio – Ladino meaning "my"

Motzi – blessing over bread

Nána – Ladino meaning "grandmother"

Niña – Ladino meaning "girl"

Niños – Ladino meaning "children"

Nóno – Ladino meaning "grandfather"

Or Ve Shalom – the name of the Sephardic synagogue in Atlanta, Georgia

Padre – Ladino meaning "father"

Paila – Ladino term for an aluminum container in which the family and the laundry were washed

Parsha – Torah portion

Patuklas – scuff-like slippers worn by traditional Sephardi women as part of their everyday dress

Pesach – Hebrew meaning "pass over," hence the English name, Passover. The spring festival commemorating both the ancient exodus from Egypt (see the book of Exodus in the Hebrew Bible) and the spring harvest.

Pita – a Middle Eastern bread that is round and hollow, often called "pocket bread" in English

Polka de samara – a velvet jacket lined with fur worn on special occasions by traditional Sephardic women

Presepio – Italian for the crèche or Nativity scene

Puerta de la Mar – Ladino meaning "Port of the Sea," the gate leading from the city to the ocean

Purim – often called in English "The Feast of Esther." A Jewish festival celebrating the ability of Queen Esther to save the Jews in ancient Persia.

Rabbi – Hebrew meaning "teacher," used to refer to the religious leader of a Jewish community

Rengrasyo te – Ladino meaning "I thank you"

Reshikas – pretzel shaped bread

Rhodelisi – a Jew from the island of Rhodes

Sal – Ladino meaning "salt"

Sayo – a cotton sheath of tunic closed at the collar with slits up to the waist worn by traditional Sephardi women as part of their everyday dress

Seder – Hebrew meaning "order," the ceremonial meal marking the beginning of Pesach.

Sephardim – Hebrew meaning "Spanish," used to refer to Jews whose ancestors are from the Iberian Peninsula

Seshicos – Ladino for cabinets

Seuda de Purim – a feast on the first day of *Purim* that traditionally included meat cooked over charcoal

Sevoyas reinadas – stuffed onions

Shabbat – Hebrew meaning "Sabbath"

Shabbat Halbashah – Ladino meaning "Sabbath of the Poor"

Shacharit – daily morning service

Shammash – Hebrew meaning "helper"

Sheshicos – a pebble mosaic floor

Shish kebabs – meat cooked on a skewer

Shvat – the 5th month of the Jewish calendar

Siddur – Hebrew meaning "prayerbook"

Siente Joya el Son de Mi Gitara – title of a Rhodelisi song, in English "Listen Julia to the Sound of my Guitar"

Sofah – a raised platform used as a bed at night and for whatever necessary during the day

Tacos – wooden clogs with a leather strap worn by women to do housework

Tallega – bag carried around a child's neck to collect sweets on *Tu B'Shvat*

Tallit – a prayer shawl used during prayer by Jews

Tanakh – Hebrew for the Hebrew Bible

Tapeties – (P.) see *tapesty*

Tapesty – Ladino term for oriental throw rugs

Tarposh – a black satin cloth used to pull back a woman's hair worn on special occasions by traditional Sephardic women

Tevah – the desk or podium from which the Torah is read

Tilia – an herb

Tiya – Ladino meaning "aunt"

Tiyo – Ladino meaning "uncle"

Tomates reinadas – stuffed tomatoes

Traife – something that is not *kosher*

Tu B'Shvat – the Jewish holiday marking the New Year of the Trees, when the trees in Israel begin to blossom again after the winter

Vos – Ladino meaning "you," as the 2nd plural person form, used by husbands when speaking to their wives

Yardan – a gold band used by traditional Sephardi women to hold their numerous necklaces together

Yazma – a scarf like head covering, of a thin printed material worn by traditional Sephardi women as part of their everyday dress

Yerno – Ladino meaning "son-in-law"